Wanderers

ON

Union Station

Book Six of EarthCent Ambassador

Wanderers on Union Station

Foner Books

ISBN 978-1-948691-08-6

Copyright 2015 by E. M. Foner

Northampton, Massachusetts

One

"In conclusion, it is the view of Union Station Embassy that the remarkable success of 'Let's Make Friends' in fostering intercultural understanding among the children of tunnel network aligned species, not to mention its jump to the top of the galactic ratings for pre-school edutainment series, is unlikely to be replicated in a new production aimed at adults, and I should therefore reject the Grenouthian offer to create a pilot for a new show."

Kelly pushed back from her display desk and wondered whether she was making a mistake. Things had been so slow around the embassy, that three years after Aisha resigned her acting junior consul position to work on her show full-time, the ambassador still hadn't requested a replacement from EarthCent. She barely had enough work to keep herself busy these days, and with Samuel starting at the Stryx school, Kelly was forced to confront the fact that she had too much free time on her hands. It was all the fault of EarthCent Intelligence, of course.

"May I say something?" Libby inquired over the office speakers.

"You already did," Kelly replied glumly, toying with her half-empty cup of coffee. Was it possible she had accidentally bought the depressant-laced version again?

"Before I send your weekly report to EarthCent, I hope I can talk you into reconsidering your conclusion," Libby said. "I think that the Grenouthian request is an interesting opportunity for you to present human culture and values to a broader audience than you could hope to reach through standard diplomatic means."

"You want me to host a grown-up version of LMF?" Kelly asked incredulously, using the acronym for Aisha's show that had caught on among the parents of preschoolers. "Am I supposed to read stories from picture books to a bunch of aliens sitting in a circle on the floor? Or maybe I'll divide them into two teams, and then I'll lie on the deck and have each team build one end of a bridge that meets over my stomach."

"That show broke the galactic record for on-demand reruns," Libby chided the ambassador. "I got a little choked up myself when that Horten boy helped the Drazen girl place the top block."

Kelly bit back the urge to say something sarcastic about AI physiology, because the truth was, she had shed a few tears herself while watching that episode with her son. In addition to being one of LMF's biggest fans, Samuel was part of the rotating cast. The show's only real critic in the house was Dorothy, and the thirteen-year-old's main objection was that none of her ideas to make the show more exciting ever got past Aisha's filter for age-appropriateness.

"Don't you think it's beneath the dignity of an ambassador to get involved in the entertainment business?" Kelly asked.

"I can name at least a dozen ambassadors on Union Station who are currently involved with immersives or the broadcast networks, including Bork," Libby replied. "And we wouldn't be having this discussion if the Grenouthian ambassador didn't own a well-deserved reputation for sniffing out new talent."

"But Bork only acts during his vacations," Kelly protested, rather feebly. "And then only in historical re-enactments. It's not like he's clowning around."

"Nobody is trying to force you to do something you don't want to do," the Stryx librarian told Kelly. "I just thought you might find time weighing a little heavy on your hands, now that I have Samuel in my school all morning and he's working with Banger in the afternoon."

"What kind of a name for a Stryx is Banger?" Kelly asked, then immediately changed her mind. "No, don't tell me. And if you hadn't manipulated us into starting an intelligence agency, I would still have more work than I could have handled. Things are so dead at the embassy these days that Donna is talking about cutting her own hours to part-time. It seems that all I've been doing the last couple years is attending official events, and I could push half of those off onto Lynx if I wanted."

"Lynx won't be the cultural attaché forever," Libby reminded her. "Blythe has cut way back on working in the two years since she had the twins, and even though her husband is well-suited for the directorship, Jeeves says that Clive would rather be doing alien archaeology."

"Now that EarthCent Intelligence is running a profit, Blythe probably figures her main job is done," Kelly replied. "And with all of the resources they've built up, I can't blame anybody for going to them for help instead of coming to the embassy. It's just that the last thing I ever expected on this job was to be under-worked and bored."

"So why don't you consider the Grenouthian offer?" Libby reiterated. "If you can't come up with a good concept that you want to be involved with, that's another matter. But it's not like you to quit without even trying."

"Why are you so gung-ho about this, Libby?" Kelly asked, with a flash of suspicion.

"I'm just concerned for a friend, and I don't want to see you waste an opportunity that you may regret later, if you aren't regretting it already," Libby replied innocently.

"I thought Jeeves was supposed to be the mind-reader," Kelly replied, a tacit admission of the accuracy of Libby's guess. "But what do I know about galactic edutainment? Aisha's show is the only thing I watch, other than the occasional Grenouthian documentary."

"But you know a lot about meeting aliens as an adult and learning to get along with them," Libby pointed out. "Remember, the rest of the species on the tunnel network have been in contact with each other for thousands of years, and in most cases, much, much longer. They take each other for granted and forget that there's still something to learn. The secret to Aisha's show is that she's very open-minded and she's learning right along with the children. Everybody senses that it's genuine."

"I'll think about it," Kelly said. "I want to talk it over with Joe and Donna. But now I guess I have to come up with a new conclusion for my weekly report."

"Why not say something about the Wanderers?" Libby suggested. "You weren't here the last time they came by Union Station since it was well before we opened Earth. I know you've received an invitation from the Wanderer envoy to their traditional arrival ceremony because Donna checked with me to make sure it was legitimate."

"I've only heard about them from the other ambassadors and Dring," Kelly objected. "I still don't understand if they're more of a political movement, or just a group of galactic drop-outs who travel from place to place as they wear out their welcome."

"The Wanderers have a continual presence in history stretching back tens of millions of years," Libby said, slipping into her professorial voice. "Their mobs include members of most of the sentient species we're aware of in this galaxy, though in some instances, their biological roots are barely recognizable to the eye, due to long periods of separation from their common ancestors."

"Could there be Gem among the Wanderers?" Kelly asked, thinking what a wonderful surprise it would be for Gwendolyn and Mist to find long-lost relatives living in the mob.

"I'm afraid not," Libby replied. "The Gem weren't advanced enough to draw a visit before they took to cloning. Although humans may think of the Wanderers as a galactic version of the gypsies back on Earth, their paths are quite different. The Wanderer mobs are so large that they are really self-contained civilizations, capable of indefinitely sustaining themselves in interstellar space if necessary. The biologicals who created the template for the Wanderers were actually explorers and colonists from a species that never developed faster-than-light travel on their own. But they were extraordinarily handy about creating sustainable environments in space using the technology they did have, and in the end, their species split between those who chose to colonize worlds and those who chose to live permanently on ships."

"Dring told me that the original Wanderers still exist, and that they are a prime example of a stable biological species," Kelly commented. "I've been looking forward to meeting them."

"It's very unlikely there are any in this particular mob," Libby said. "The original Wanderers still eschew faster-than-light travel, since they view it as cheating. This mob began arriving through a one-time tunnel early in the week, a sort of an intermediate technology between jump drives and the permanent tunnel network we maintain. From what Gryph tells me, most of the ships coming in are from species you're already familiar with, though of course, there's usually a cultural split between those who join a mob and those who don't."

"How many people are there in this, uh, mob?"

"Do you mean humans or sentients?"

"Well, I meant sentients, but are you saying there are humans among them?" Kelly asked.

"It's difficult to predict the final size of a Wanderer mob before they all arrive. Sometimes they come from different locations according to a prior arrangement, but this mob will clearly include millions of individuals, a small number of whom are human," Libby replied.

"How can humans have ended up with the Wanderers when we've been in space less than a hundred years?"

"Between labor contracts and the tunnel network, humanity has spread much more thinly and rapidly than biologicals who develop interstellar space travel on their own," Libby explained. "And your polyglot home culture, including hundreds of national identities, makes humans more comfortable living with other species than sentients who reached cultural homogeneity before venturing into space."

"It sounds to me like a Wanderer mob is a sort of utopia for inter-species relations," Kelly mused. "I don't mean to belittle your achievements with the tunnel network, but face it. Some of the aliens on this station would be at each other's throats if the Stryx weren't in charge."

"I'm sure the Wanderers get some things correct," Libby replied, sounding slightly miffed. "But I think you'll find that their utopia lives up to its literal meaning."

"Is it true that they steal children from the places they visit to build their population?" Kelly asked.

"Not in the sense that humans use child-theft," Libby replied. "I don't want to spoil all the surprises for you before you get a chance to visit the mob in person."

"Won't they be coming onto Union Station as well?"

"Gryph and the rest of the first generation Stryx have long enforced a strict policy to limit the number of Wanderers they'll allow on a station at one time," Libby replied. "There have been incidents in the past that we don't want to see repeated."

"You're speaking pretty mysteriously for a reference librarian," Kelly complained. "Why do I get the feeling that you're setting me up for something?"

"Joe's here," Libby announced, just before the door to Kelly's office whooshed open.

Dorothy and Samuel both made it through the door before their father, who followed after them with a bottle in a paper bag gripped by the neck in one hand.

"We came to get you because Daddy said you'd forget," Dorothy announced before Samuel could catch his breath.

"Can Banger come, Mommy?" the five-year-old boy pleaded. "He said he never gets to eat dinner."

"Stryx don't eat," Dorothy reminded her younger brother in a weary tone. "And they don't have to protect their eyes when somebody is welding because they aren't really eyes. Banger isn't a biological, you know."

"Bye-logical?" Samuel repeated. Dorothy just rolled her eyes and started playing with her mother's display desk.

"What did I forget?" Kelly asked Joe.

Without looking up, Dorothy answered before her father could. "We're eating dinner with Ambassador Gem and Mist," she said. "Aisha and Paul are at some Grenouthian network event. There! Mist holo'd me the main course."

"Turkey," Joe said, patting his stomach in anticipation after the hologram appeared over the display desk. "They must have ordered out from Fowl Territory, the new place in the Little Apple everybody is talking about. I hope Gwen has invited some other families, or she and Mist will be eating turkey all week."

"You'll have to ask Aunty Gwen if Banger can come, it's her house," Kelly told Samuel. The boy grabbed his mother's hand and started pulling her towards the door. "And you'll have to be patient. I haven't finished my weekly report yet."

"Is my implant time running fast?" Joe asked. "I thought I had your Friday schedule down to a science."

"Well, I actually did my weekly, but Libby talked me out of posting it," Kelly admitted. "She thinks I should give more consideration to the Grenouthian proposal that I produce a show promoting inter-species understanding, though you know the bunnies only care about the ratings."

"Our own show?" Dorothy exclaimed, suddenly interested in the conversation. "I have lots of ideas."

"Just hold onto them until dinner, Dot," Kelly replied quickly. "In fact, why don't you all go on ahead without me and I'll catch up in a few minutes, just as soon as I finish the report."

"Alright," Dorothy said, deciding for the family before the others could offer their opinions. "But don't be too late, because Mist and I are babysitting for the twins later."

"You just turned thirteen, and Blythe has you working at night? I don't like it," Kelly objected, looking towards Joe for support.

"I seem to remember Blythe selling me flowers late at night in the Little Apple when she was younger than Dorothy, and Chastity couldn't have been much more than ten," Joe replied unhelpfully. "Besides, Mist is getting to be a responsible adult."

"I'm a responsible adult too," Dorothy declared, as she herded her younger brother out the door. "Just not all of the time."

"You see the problems you cause?" Kelly directed her accusation at the ceiling after the door slid shut behind her family. "And how come the co-owner of InstaSitter uses her mother and my daughter to do her babysitting? Doesn't she trust her own service?"

"Donna would pay to babysit her grandchildren if Clive would let her, and Blythe pays Dorothy and Mist directly to cut out my overhead commission," Libby explained. "Have you decided on a new conclusion for your report?"

"I haven't had time to think," Kelly muttered, feeling something akin to writer's block. "If Gryph and the other Stryx think the Wanderers are such a bad influence that they have a quota for letting them on the stations, why welcome them at all?"

"In a sense the Wanderers represent an alternative to the tunnel network. Even if we don't always approve of their lifestyle, they offer an important back-up should something unforeseen occur."

"What do you mean, Libby? Are they that technologically advanced that they can support the Stryx in an emergency?"

"Not at all," Libby replied in exasperation. "Wanderer technology is derived from the constituent species of the mob, along with whatever they may pick up along the way as gifts. For example, the temporary tunnels this mob employs are created by a pair of robotic ships supplied to them by Stryx Dreel many millions of years ago."

"So how do they support you as a back-up?" Kelly doggedly pursued the issue.

"Unintentionally," Libby said, after an uncharacteristically long pause. "I don't want to tell you more, because while not technically a secret, it touches on subjects that the advanced species tend to suppress within their own cultures for psychological reasons, meaning there's a sort of competitive advantage involved."

"Fine!" Kelly snorted "Hide behind your phony noninterference principles and manipulate me into figuring it out for myself later. Now let's finish recording my report so I can get to dinner."

"I'm ready," Libby said calmly. "Do you need me to play back what you said just before the conclusion?"

"Please," Kelly replied, realizing she had no recall of the rest of the report whatsoever.

The embassy manager reports that we're running out of paperclips again, and that we can't obtain any in the local markets because the aliens don't use paper. In fact, we're running low on Post-it notes as well, the kind that don't leave a sticky residue on tabs. And pencils, though I can probably get those through EarthCent Intelligence since they use them for secure messages. There really hasn't been much going on lately, though I received

a request from the Grenouthian ambassador to create a new show
for their network, something along the lines of my former acting
junior consul's show, but aimed at adults.

"That was really me?" Kelly asked, after listening to her own voice played back. "I used my weekly report to complain about office supplies?"

"Before that, you went on for some length on the subject of creating a standard uniform for EarthCent ambassadors, including a hat," Libby told her. "Do you want to hear it?"

"I want you to erase it!" Kelly exclaimed. "What's happening to me? My reports used to be the gold standard at EarthCent. They even used them in the training course!"

"I'm sure it's just the sudden change with Samuel starting school," Libby reassured the ambassador. "Would you like me to encrypt the current report so that it can't be decoded, and if they get around to asking about it, I'll say that it was an experiment and that I lost the key?"

"You'd lie for me, Libby?" Kelly asked.

"Of course," the Stryx librarian replied. "You're my friend."

"Then encrypt and send," Kelly said with relief. "I'll work on an idea for the Grenouthians this weekend. I guess I do need a new project."

"Don't we all," Libby said to herself, as Kelly headed off to catch up with her family.

Two

"So, are we attending as the EarthCent cultural attaché and escort, or as spies?" Thomas asked Lynx this question as they waited for the shuttle that would take them out to the Wanderer mob.

"Well, as the attaché and escort, I guess, though everybody knows it means the same thing," Lynx replied. "Have you ever come across these Wanderers before?"

"When would I have had the chance?" Thomas asked. "You keep forgetting that I'm not even half your age, and I've spent practically my whole life on Union Station."

"Right," Lynx replied, watching as the returning shuttle whisked through the atmospheric retention field protecting Union Station's excursion platform for nitrogen/oxygen breathers. The small craft that were usually rented by sightseers to tour the outside of the station were now employed shuttling station inhabitants back and forth to the visiting ships of the mob. For some reason, Gryph wouldn't allow the Wanderers to establish their own shuttle service, but local small craft owners like Joe were working around the clock as casual space taxis.

"I've been watching the mob arrive over the station feed, and I saw that one of the ships is designated as a dance hall," Thomas said. "I sort of promised Chastity that I'd check it out for her."

"It's probably as good a place to start as any," Lynx replied. "When I asked Libby how long the mob would be here, she said, 'Too long,' so I guess we don't have to hurry to do our survey."

"I'm especially curious to see if the species all live together or if they mainly stick to their own ships," Thomas said, as they boarded the shuttle. "I've been reading through everything I could find about the Wanderers and it isn't at all clear. It's almost as if nobody thinks they're worth studying."

"I'm not really sure they are," Lynx said. "I traded with some Wanderers out on the Drazen frontier maybe ten years ago. They were from a relatively small mob, and I didn't accept their invitation to come out and visit because, well, I'd heard things about them. You know?"

Thomas frowned and shook his head. "I don't know. What kind of things?"

"Like single women going out to visit a mob, sending messages back to their families that they were happy there, and then disappearing for years, if not forever."

"Did you hear anything about artificial people going missing?" Thomas asked, sounding concerned.

"I don't think so, but I probably wouldn't have remembered if I had," Lynx replied. "Besides, they're in Stryx jurisdiction here, so I can't imagine they'll try anything."

"But you still invited me along," Thomas pointed out.

"It's your job, too," Lynx retorted. "I would have asked Woojin, but he's taking turns with Paul and Joe flying the Nova as a shuttle. They're working three shifts."

"Why didn't we go with them?" Thomas asked, pausing before he strapped himself into the acceleration seat.

"They wouldn't have accepted our money," Lynx replied. "You know how Blythe and Clive feel about not muddling up work-related expenses. By the way, if you can't use your programmable cred for something, remember to ask for a receipt."

"There's nothing in my personality enhancement to suggest that spies ever ask for receipts," Thomas grumbled.

"That's because your personality enhancement was based on fictional works," Lynx reminded him. "Do you think that the traveling salesman cover story would hold water if you ran around spending cash on everything?"

"Are you two really spies?" asked a little Horten boy, who was sitting with his mother on the facing pair of acceleration seats. The Horten matron turned pale with embarrassment.

"We sure are," Thomas replied kindly. "Do you want to sign up as a double agent? I have a badge around here somewhere."

Before he could find it, the shuttle completed loading, and the chairs all pivoted around to face the front of the ship. Immediately after it cleared the atmosphere retention field under its own power, Gryph took over with manipulator fields, as he did for all of the shipping traffic in the station core. The ship accelerated smoothly all through its passage of the long core, and by the time it emerged beyond the station, it was moving so fast that it had to follow a gentle looping course to approach the mob.

There was a brief moment's weightlessness at the halfway point of the journey, during which the shuttle rotated in space to point its main engines towards the mob and began to decelerate. The whole trip lasted about twenty minutes.

"Welcome to the Phygorean Mob transportation hub," a voice intoned as they emerged from the shuttle. "We offer shared-taxi service to all of the vessels that are receiving guests, free of charge. This hub is a Zero-G environment, so if you don't have magnetic cleats or a companion to tow you, wait near your shuttle and an attendant will be along shortly. Please note that shared taxis will only depart when all of the seats are taken or three Zarents have expired. Private taxi service to all destinations is also available."

"Was that in English or translated?" Lynx whispered to Thomas. She held onto her partner's elbow as she clicked her heels to activate her magnetic cleats. At times she really missed her old trader implant, which did a good enough job without confusing her brain as to what was actually going on. The translation through the diplomatic implant supplied by EarthCent Intelligence was so seamless that she didn't know what language was being spoken unless she could watch the speaker's lips.

"It was Verlock, oddly enough," Thomas informed her. "It was speeded up by a factor of three, but definitely Verlock. Hey, where did that little boy go? I found a badge."

"Too late," Lynx said. "They bolted the second the safety locks came off. My guess is that the free shared-taxi service isn't any great bargain if you get stuck waiting around for three Zarents, however long that is. I wonder why my implant didn't translate the time units?"

"Zarents aren't a unit of time, they're a species that's dedicated to deep space maintenance work," Thomas explained. "I don't think they even have a home world, they just live with Wanderer mobs and other permanent fleets."

"So when they said a shared service would only depart with empty seats after three Zarents expired...?"

"I think we should splurge on a private taxi," Thomas replied significantly.

Lynx and her artificial partner glide-stepped their way out of the shuttle, which was moored haphazardly to a pier just inside one of the least-convincing atmospheric retention fields the former trader had ever seen. The so-called transportation hub was basically a big metal box filled with air and pierced at regular intervals with portals for arriving and departing craft. Holographic representations of the more popular vessels in the mob appeared above various shared-taxi stands and empty slips, but the majority of the arriving visitors were queued in line at the paid stand.

"Paradise? Paradise?" a young Drazen inquired, working his way along the queue. "Just two short for the shared service to Paradise. Come on, give it a try. How about you two?" he asked, stopping right in front of Lynx.

"No thanks," Lynx replied. "We're going to Dance Hall."

"Dance Hall is lame," the young Drazen told them. "You can dance in Paradise too, plus there are all sorts of opportunities for, you know—can't spell humanoid without M-A-N."

"That's a very penetrating observation for such a young Drazen, but we have prior plans," Lynx replied.

"Hey, I was just being nice," the Drazen retorted. "I don't usually go for older chicks."

Thomas held Lynx back as the young Drazen resumed his search for fares to get the shared service moving.

"Older chicks?" Lynx fumed. "Let go of me and I'll show that Drazen brat who the chick is."

"Take it easy, partner," Thomas soothed her. "He's probably been waiting for hours to save a few creds on the ride. Didn't you have money problems when you were his age?"

"His age?" Lynx turned her fury on the artificial person. "First you tell me that I'm twice as old as you, and now this punk who probably has more notches in his tentacle than I ever will is supposed to be a younger generation? I'm barely thirty."

"If you say so," Thomas agreed noncommittally. "Wow, this is one of the fastest lines I've ever been in."

Lynx swallowed her indignation and peered around the large Dollnick couple who were shuffling along in front of them. Sure enough, they were just a couple steps from the gate where taxis were continually halting, disgorging passengers, and taking on new fares.

"Where to?" a scruffy-looking human asked from the pilot's seat of his short-hop space taxi.

"Dance Hall," Thomas responded quickly, in case Lynx was having second thoughts about the whole thing.

"Hop in," the driver said.

Lynx and Thomas stepped over the sill and strapped themselves in with the loose harnesses on the bench seat. As soon as the transparent bubble closed over the passenger compartment, the taxi-stand operator triggered the magnetic catapult to fling the little craft into space.

"Shouldn't you start the meter?" Lynx asked politely.

"Nah, I'll give you a deal," the driver said. "How does fifty creds sound?"

"Do you accept programmable creds?" Thomas inquired.

"Sure thing," the driver replied. "Just stick it in the mini-register slot in the back there."

"Wait a second," Lynx said, grabbing her partner's wrist before he could insert the coin supplied by EarthCent

Intelligence for paying salary and covering expenses. "Fifty creds is at least twice what a little jaunt like this should cost. Do we look like a couple of dumb kids to you?"

"Fifty creds is fair for Dance Hall," the driver replied sulkily. "If you're going to be cheapskates about it, I can do forty-five, but I won't make a dime after paying the company."

"Cut the big act and turn on the meter," Lynx said, becoming annoyed with the driver's persistence. "We both know perfectly well that the mini-register back here isn't taxi equipment, it's your personal currency holder. If you don't want to do things legal, then take us back to the hub and we'll get another cab."

"I can't start the meter now, we're halfway there already," the driver protested, changing tack. "Look, thirty creds and it'll be the best bargain you ever made. Just wait until you catch a cab back later and you'll find out what a great deal you got."

"Start the meter," Lynx demanded, her voice turning cold. She nudged her partner and gestured with her chin.

"Yeah, start the meter," Thomas repeated, this time employing one of the command voices that came with his secret agent personality upgrade.

"This is what's wrong with humanity," the man whined, turning on the meter. "Nobody trusts anybody anymore. Now I've wasted my lunch break to make more money for my boss, and who's going to make that right for me?"

"I checked the time when we left the hub and I'll add on the difference when we arrive at Dance Hall," Lynx said, relenting a little. "But don't take us on a grand tour of the mob. I can see Dance Hall from here, and the fastest way between two points is a straight line."

The driver cheered up a bit when Lynx mentioned making up the difference, since she'd be paying for off-meter time that he could embezzle out of the cash box without coming up short. Before another two minutes passed, they were entering the core of Dance Hall, which looked like an enormous spoked donut from space. The AI handling traffic that entered through the spinning habitat's axis caught the taxi in its manipulator fields and quickly spun it up to Dance Hall's rotational speed for docking at the taxi stand.

"Alright, the meter says nine creds, so adding the time you spent trying to con us, I figure we owe fourteen," Lynx said. "Just tell the real mini-register that we're offering a five-cred tip."

The driver's only reply was to speak the figure to the taxi's meter, which immediately extruded a mini-register slot of its own from an articulated arm that pivoted around to the back bench. Thomas inserted his programmable coin, confirmed the amount, and received it back, fourteen creds lighter. The two humans exited the cab, and the taxi-stand controller moved it forward to the departures gate, where new fares were waiting to get ripped-off.

"How did you know he was overcharging us so badly?" Thomas asked.

"How could you not know?" Lynx asked in reply, though it was hard to be irritated with her partner's lack of trading sense when she was still basking in the glow of vindication. "Nobody ever gives you a deal off-meter. It's just how dishonesty works. Once they decide to cheat their boss, why would they do their passengers a favor?"

"There's the lift tube," Thomas said, guiding Lynx through the crowd of exhausted revelers on their way home. "From what I read, practically all of the ships in the mob are like miniature versions of Union Station, spinning cylinders with multiple decks that simulate gravity with angular acceleration. But Dance Hall is more of a flat ring, just one giant dance floor, though the curvature is probably obvious unless the ceiling is really high."

"I'll be glad to get down to the dance floor," Lynx admitted. "I never would have thought it possible back when I was trading, but I think I'm beginning to lose my space legs."

"What do you mean?" Thomas asked, as the lift accelerated outwards, giving Lynx the feeling that she was oriented with her feet in the wrong direction.

"Zero-G, I'm not used to it anymore," Lynx complained. "I've barely been off Union Station since I took this job. For ten years before that, I practically lived in space on my two-man trader."

"Why didn't I think of that?" Thomas exclaimed. "We should have taken your ship and saved on the shuttle and taxi fare."

"I had Gryph move it to off-station parking for me last year," Lynx told him, and then sighed. "It's basically mothballed. I doubt I even remember how to fly it."

"I could teach you," Thomas offered helpfully. "I watched you back on our first mission and I never forget anything."

"Except the time." Lynx elbowed him playfully, feeling better as the increasing distance from the core gave her a more definite sense of up and down. "Wow, look at all those people."

The EarthCent Intelligence operatives found themselves descending towards a mass of dancing sentients, only slightly distorted through the transparent cylindrical walls of the capsule and shaft. A rainbow of low-intensity lasers bounced off of clouds of mirror balls suspended from the ceiling, making it difficult to accurately identify the species of the dancers in different sections, even as they drew closer. Only when the capsule halted at the floor, and then separated like a bell jar to allow the passengers to exit, did an obnoxiously loud mix of techno-music overwhelm the new arrivals.

"This isn't real dancing," Thomas shouted to Lynx in disappointment. "They're just jumping around like the floor is too hot, and waving their arms like they're under attack by biting insects."

"It's so huge, there must be other dances going on," Lynx shouted back. "We must have missed a map or something."

"You're right!" Thomas yelled in reply, looking much more cheerful. "Bring up the information channel on your implant."

Lynx blinked a few times and made some selections with practiced movements of her left pupil, even though she could have navigated faster by just subvocing. For some reason, she liked doing things the old-fashioned way. When she reached the standard information channel used by markets, museums and spaceports around the galaxy, a detailed map appeared. It included the standard "You are here," arrow, and a graphical breakdown showing the different dances currently going on.

"Argentine tango is right out at the end," she remarked loudly, counting on her partner's ability to separate her voice from the background noise. "Wait a second. They have a tango going on at the other end as well."

"It's really just one dance, they cut it in half to create a flat projection for the map," Thomas replied, bending to speak directly in Lynx's ear. "We took exactly the wrong lift tube and came down opposite from where we need to be. Do you want to hoof it, or should we go back up and then down again?"

"We're here to do research, so we may as well walk," Lynx replied, looking doubtfully at the slow curvature of the floor. "How far do you think it is?"

"Maybe a half an hour if we can find a clear lane," Thomas responded. "Follow me. I'm taking the shortest path off of this alleged dance floor."

Lynx fell in behind Thomas, who was using his shoulders and elbows in a much more energetic fashion than she had ever seen him do before. Either he was in a genuine hurry to get to the tango, or the weird music and the spastic dance moves really bothered him.

Three

Dring was the last of the invited guests to arrive at the brainstorming session Kelly had set up to discuss show ideas for the Grenouthian network. She wondered idly if it was some kind of galactic rule that the sentients with the longest commute showed up first, since Czeros had been almost fifteen minutes early. Then again, the Frunge ambassador had problems at home, and he could be counted on to show up early anywhere that alcohol was on offer.

"Thank you all for coming," Kelly said, surveying the living area of the ice harvester with a sudden lump in her throat. During the first half of her career working for EarthCent, the diplomatic service had moved her about constantly, so she rarely stayed at any posting for more than a year. She was sure that she must have made friends during that period, but after fifteen years on Union Station, she couldn't remember any of them.

Donna and her husband sat on the couch with Czeros, Gwendolyn was in one of the easy chairs, Bork and his wife Shinka occupied the new love-seat, and Dring, as was his habit, remained standing in preference to crushing his tail. Joe was in the basement drawing a fresh pitcher of his latest homebrewed Pilsner to test on the guests, and Beowulf was sprawled on the throw rug, gnawing the latest in chew-toy technology. The faux bone was a new novelty item that Peter Hadad was considering for Kitchen Kitsch, and Beowulf had volunteered as the quality tester.

"So, here's the challenge," Kelly said. "You all know that the Grenouthians have asked me to come up with a new edutainment series to foster interspecies relations, and even though I know they're just in it for the advertising revenue, I think it could be a great opportunity for EarthCent to expand its diplomatic brand."

"Brand?" Joe asked. He placed the pitcher on the coffee table for self-service and settled into the remaining easy chair.

"I met with the, er, younger set over at the EarthCent Intelligence offices for lunch today to get their opinions," Kelly confessed. "Shaina and Blythe started talking about market positioning and branding, and when they found out that Aisha is only getting a ten-percent royalty from the Grenouthians on her Hindu dancer action figure, the whole discussion went off the rails. Then they got onto the subject of the Wanderer mob and Paul offered to take everybody out to visit in the Nova, so that was the end of that."

"Never a good idea to hold a meeting outside of your own territory," Czeros informed her. "You lose control of the agenda."

"Be that as it may, I think there could be a real upside for EarthCent if we can attract even a fraction of the attention from adults that Aisha's show is getting from children," Kelly replied. "I mean, for those of us here, our jobs bring all of us in close contact with the other species. And even the station residents who stick to their own decks are only a couple minutes in a lift tube away from what amounts to a different world. But most of the

24

sentients in the galaxy, even on the tunnel network, live on worlds and colonies with homogenous populations."

"The Grenouthian documentaries are already one of the most popular forms of entertainment in the galaxy," Shinka reminded her. "I'm always getting questions from relatives back home about whether the humans still go on slaving raids, refuse to bathe for fear of getting sick, or build giant tombs from stone and kill all the workers."

"What do you tell them?" Stanley asked.

"Oh, I just laugh and suggest that they visit for themselves," Shinka replied. "Bork tells me that Earth can use the tourist traffic."

"But this is exactly what I'm getting at," Kelly exclaimed. "The Grenouthian documentaries are sensationalistic, that's why everybody watches them. I want to come up with a show that teaches viewers something about the other species as they really are today, not cherry-pick the low-lights from their history for the sake of cheap thrills."

"So what did you have in mind?" Gwendolyn asked. Serving as the Gem ambassador for three years had built her self-confidence to the point that Kelly barely recognized the former waitress clone whose most-used phrase had been, "I'm sorry."

"I don't have anything in mind, that's why I called for a brainstorming session," Kelly admitted.

"My implant translated the term you're using as describing an archaic methodology for group problem-solving based on one of several approaches," Bork said. "I asked Libby for details, and she said there were a number of techniques for brainstorming, including a version where only one person in the room knows the specifics of the problem up for solution, and another version where nobody knows. It sounded a bit like a Drazen party game."

"It's too late for either of those approaches," Donna pointed out. "We all know what the goal is, to come up with a grown-up version of Aisha's show, which is really Kelly and Aisha's show, if you go back to the creation."

"Then the logical thing to do is to analyze what parts of Let's Make Friends work for adults," Dring said. "Once we've distilled the essence that can be transferred, we can start thinking about possibilities for a new framework."

"That's a great idea," Kelly declared. "I realize that most of you have probably only watched a little out of curiosity, since it's intended for preschoolers, but it would be really valuable to know if there are some universal elements. How about we go in a circle, starting with you, Peter?"

"Well, I don't mind going first, but I never really watched the whole show," the Hadad patriarch said. "I think the dance bit she opens with is brilliant, and I know that sari sales on the Shuk deck have gone from nothing to hundreds of outfits a day since the show became popular. The Dollnicks are selling knock-offs already."

"Thank you, Peter," Kelly said. "Joe?"

"I like the sock puppets," Joe said unashamedly. "And the toy of the week segment, where a sponsor donates a new toy being introduced to the market? That's hilarious. Even the kids from the species the toy is designed for usually prefer playing with the packaging."

"Sock puppets and empty boxes," Kelly scribbled on a yellow legal pad, the latest retro affectation sweeping the human deck. "Dring?"

"The word of the day," Dring said decisively, "If any of you haven't seen it, that's where she asks the children on each show for the latest word they learned, and then they pick the most interesting one for her to research for the next episode."

"I didn't know Aisha was a linguist," Peter commented.

"She's not," Kelly replied. "She just comes home and asks Dring, who probably makes up the etymologies."

"I haven't been caught yet," the little dinosaur responded with a toothy grin.

"Donna?" Kelly asked.

"What I like most about the show is that Blythe's twins stay still for it," Donna said. "I don't think they understand much of what's going on, but when all the little aliens join the story circle with Aisha, the twins move right into the hologram and sit quietly, as if they were in the studio."

"Hmm, holographic participation," Kelly said, writing on her pad. "That might carry over."

"That and the sock puppets," Donna added.

"Stanley?" Kelly asked.

"I like the whole living sets and numbers concept," Stanley replied. "I know it's corny, but when she put a bunch of little humanoids together in one set, a Chert, a Frunge and a human, and then she made another set out of a Dollnick, a Verlock and a Grenouthian, all of the young aliens learned that the two sets were equal, even though one took up twice as much space as the other. Of course, the Drazen child was the first one to get the right answer, since it's easy to compare three and three when you have six fingers on each hand."

"I don't see how we can work basic counting into a show for adults," Kelly said.

"There's racing odds," Joe suggested, drawing a dark look from his wife.

"Czeros?" Kelly asked.

"You know I have several little shrubs at home, and although their mother is, shall we say, slightly xenophobic, she can't keep them from watching," the Frunge replied. "I tend to be elsewhere during the broadcasts, but I have to admit that the theme song is rather catchy. The children insist I sing it when I plant them for the night." He began to clear his throat in preparation to performing the tune.

"Thank you, Ambassador," Kelly cut him off diplomatically. "Perhaps we'll have a sing-along when we finish getting everybody's input. Gwen?"

"I watch it every day," the Gem ambassador confessed. "The children are so cute that I wish I could take them all home."

"Is there anything about the show itself that appeals to you?" Kelly asked.

"Oh, I like it all, especially the sock puppets," Gwendolyn said.

Kelly put a double underline beneath "sock puppets" on her legal pad. "Bork?"

"You know our children are all grown, so I've only seen the show once or twice when babysitting their offspring," Bork replied. "My favorite part is where Aisha has the children ask each other questions. It's interesting to learn what children don't know and what they're curious about. I've observed that more than half of the questions are about food, and bedtime ran a strong second. On one show," he continued, growing somewhat excited, "a little Verlock asked the other children if they thought he talked normally, and they all agreed he was too slow. But then on a different show, the little Drazen asked all of the other children if it hurt when their tentacles were cut off. In fact, I think I saw a Dollnick kid ask the same question about arms on a different occasion, but you know they change the children on the show every eleven episodes, so similar questions repeat..." Bork trailed off, looking around self-consciously. "Well, maybe I've been babysitting more than I realized."

"Asking each other questions," Kelly said out loud, as she wrote it down. "Shinka?"

"I would have sworn that the show is usually on during your office hours," the Drazen ambassador's wife said to her husband. "I can't offer such a detailed breakdown myself, but I do like the sock puppets, and the explanations the children give about their clothing are fascinating. I never would have guessed that Frunge children wear shoes to keep the dirt in."

"It's the best way to get the essential minerals when you're young," Czeros explained. "It's not just any dirt. They sell a special mixture at the market."

"I guess that just leaves me," Kelly said, looking around the room. Beowulf raised his head and scowled. "I'm sorry, me and the overgrown hound. Do you have something to say?"

Beowulf rose, shook himself, and then did an elaborate downward-dog stretch, keeping his eyes on Kelly the whole time. Kelly shook her head, and he repeated the movement.

"You like the stretching exercises?" Joe guessed. Beowulf nodded his head enthusiastically, and then sauntered out of the room and down the ramp for one of his periodic patrols around Mac's Bones.

"Yoga," Kelly said, writing it on the pad irritably. "That was what I was going to say." She paused for a minute and thought. "I guess I like the sock puppets too, and the introductions Aisha does when they change children on the show."

"Are there any snacks?" Bork asked, receiving an elbow in the ribs from his wife.

"Oh, I'm sorry, I forgot to put them out," Kelly exclaimed. "Can you get them, Joe? Paul and Aisha took Samuel out to see the Wanderers with the rest of that bunch, and I guess I was worried about the rumors and got a little absent minded."

"Chastity has been going out to the mob every evening to dance, and she doesn't even come home some nights," Donna said in sympathy. "I'm beginning to wonder if their reputation for child-stealing isn't well deserved."

"She's twenty-four years old," Stanley pointed out. "Chas can take care of herself. It's those Wanderers who better keep their eyes open."

"I made Paul invite Jeeves along," Kelly confessed. "I still worry, though. Maybe it will be better after I meet their envoy at the dinner next week, when the mob finally finishes arriving."

"I had no idea there would be so many," Joe said, parking the food service trolley he'd recently fabricated from spare parts. "There must be over a thousand vessels out there already, and many of them are repurposed colony ships. There could be more Wanderers in that mob than there are sentients on the station."

Bork and Czeros immediately rose and attacked the finger food, and Beowulf suddenly reappeared. Joe hadn't noticed earlier when the Huravian hound had artfully deformed one of the trolley's casters with his massive jaw power, so the bearings now made a high frequency squeal that the dog could hear from all the way across the hold.

"Maybe the Wanderers will have some good ideas for a show," Kelly said pointedly. The guests turned back to her. "Now the way I see it, the consensus choice for the best element was sock puppets, but I don't know how we can use that. The word-of-the-day has potential, the explanations about clothing and other common items could be interesting, and I like the concept of contestants questioning each other."

"Wait, what contestants?" Donna asked. "They're little children, and the whole point of the show is how well they get along with each other. Sometimes I see Aisha as more of a playmate for them than a host."

"That's a great idea!" Peter said. "A sort of a game show where the host is one of the contestants, and they ask each other questions about their species."

"Maybe not their species, but their cultures," Shinka chimed in enthusiastically. "I'd love to ask some humans about their cooking and some Dollnicks about their investments."

"I'd like to ask some aliens how they come up with their technologies, and how the stuff actually works," Joe said. "How did the Frunge ever invent those wing sets, and how come none of my torches will cut through the sheet metal the Verlocks use to build cheap shipping containers?"

"I just use scissors," Dring told him. "But I do wonder why the artificial people I meet always wear the clothes of the species that created them. I'd like to ask a few, but the ones on the station always look so busy."

"Probably hustling to pay off their body mortgages," Stanley commented.

"Did we just come up with an idea for a show?" Kelly asked in wonder. She looked down at her legal pad where she had been scribbling away unconsciously, almost like a form of automatic writing. In addition to the ideas just floated by her friends, she had written QUIZ SHOW in capital letters and drawn a circle around it. "Quiz Show?"

31

"These are really good sandwiches," Bork said, looking over from the food trolley. "Did I miss anything?"

"You missed our brainstorm," Shinka told her husband.

"You couldn't wait for me?" Bork asked incredulously. "I even saved you some of that stinky cheese that you like."

"No, you didn't," Czeros mumbled guiltily, his mouth full.

"There's more in the kitchen," Kelly said. "I know better than to put everything out at once when there are diplomats around."

Four

When the band went on break, Chastity returned to the table where Blythe and Clive were sipping their drinks. Chance remained on the dance floor another five minutes, working on new moves to music only she could hear.

"I just love Dance Hall," Chance said, her eyes sparking like Van Der Graaf generators when she finally retook her seat. "I think I'm going to run away with the Wanderers when they leave."

"Wouldn't you miss Thomas?" Chastity asked her.

"Sure," Chance replied, looking uncomfortable. "But he'd still be here when I got back, we don't age the same way as biologicals. Besides, it's not like we could make a baby if I stayed."

"I'm sure Libby told me that artificial people could produce offspring," Blythe said.

"Well, we can, but it's messy," Chance admitted, toying with the grain alcohol Clive had thoughtfully ordered for her.

"Try having twins the old-fashioned way before you talk to me about messy," Blythe remonstrated. Clive reached over and rubbed his wife's back, looking pleased with himself over his part in their fruitful union.

"So, who did you get to watch Thing One and Thing Two tonight?" Chastity asked.

33

"Lynx," Clive replied, as Blythe glowered at her sister. "She volunteered."

"Why don't you just use InstaSitter?" Chance asked. "Has the business failed?"

"Because we're blacklisted!" Blythe replied angrily. "When we set up InstaSitter, we made a rule that if three consecutive babysitters requested to be relieved of their duties, we put a hold on the client. The twins burned through three sitters in one night, though I suspect somebody intentionally assigned the most delicate employees available," she concluded loudly.

"Don't bother trying to put the blame on Libby, she can't hear you on this ship," Chastity said.

"I wouldn't bet on that," Blythe retorted. "It's not like I was calling for babysitters all the time, either. One night a week. Everybody says it's healthy to take a break."

"How come we couldn't get your mother or Dorothy to sit?" Clive asked.

"Mom is running her monthly EarthCent mixer tonight, and Dorothy had some school thing with Mist that the McAllisters all went to see, so that eliminated Aisha and Kelly as well." Blythe ticked off the possibilities on her fingers. "Shaina and Brinda are off doing an auction on one of the stations with Jeeves, and Thomas took an informal gig as a dance instructor at the mixers. Lynx was with Thomas when I pinged him, so she volunteered. She's never sat for the Things before."

"Don't let your sister train you into calling our children Things as well," Clive said. "They're just rambunctious two-year-olds with a well-developed sense of play."

"I debriefed the InstaSitters they chased off," Chastity mentioned matter-of-factly. "The twins tag-teamed them, 'relentless' was the word the Verlock sitter used, and they're tough as nails."

"It's just a phase," Clive insisted. "Hey, Chas. That guy you were dancing with earlier is coming over."

"Really?" Chastity asked. She fought the urge to turn around and look, sat up a little straighter, and smoothed her elegant tango dress at the same time. "How do I look?"

"You look beautiful," Chance told her. "Speaking of which, I'm going back to work. I can't goof off all night with my employers right here."

EarthCent Intelligence's femme fatale agent rose from her chair and headed off in the direction of the adjacent dance floor, where a Horten Mosh was going full-force. Unlike Thomas, Chance was equally at home with alien music and dance steps, and she had even been known to extract information from Vergallians on their home turf, all without the help of pheromones.

"Is this seat open?" asked the tall human, who was dressed in a well-tailored silk suit and patent leather shoes. With his curly dark hair, nearly-black eyes and narrow build, he reminded Clive vaguely of a mercenary who had broken his contract and disappeared with the platoon's monthly supply of boots, a mystery that had never been solved or explained.

"Yes it is, Marcus," Chastity answered a little too quick-ly, and then blushed, a rare occurrence for a Doogal girl. "Do you think the band will start again soon, or are they bringing in a new group?"

"Let's see," Marcus said, consulting a heads-up display through his implant that was invisible to the others. "This is the mandatory long break, helps with the drinks busi-ness. If you prefer to dance continually for hours on end, we'll have to come for one of the cover-charge periods when they play straight through."

Blythe shot Clive a significant look at the newcomer's invitation to Chastity and gave him their private interrogation signal.

"It's a pleasure to meet you, Marcus," Clive said, half rising from his chair and extending a hand across the table. "I noticed you dancing with my sister-in-law earlier. This is my wife, Blythe."

"Ah, I thought the two of you looked related," Marcus said to Blythe, as he leaned forward and shook Clive's hand. "I was trying to calculate the odds that Chastity was on the Intrepid and we'd never met, but that I'd have missed you both doesn't seem arithmetically possible."

"We're just out for the evening from Union Station," Clive informed him. "But the Intrepid rings a bell. Wasn't Intrepid the name of a colony ship commune from the first big contract expiration?"

"That's right," Marcus replied. "I'm surprised anybody remembers those times, you must be something of a historian. My parents were part of the 'Hands and Minds,' labor pool that signed those twenty-year contracts with the Dollnicks. Their group had an option to take their pay as a repurposed colony ship if they met all of their quotas. Of course, nobody understood back then that without a destination a colony ship is no bargain, but they made the best of it."

"I seem to remember reading that the Intrepid commune voted to use the ship as a base for asteroid mining off the tunnel network. Is that where they disappeared to?" Clive asked.

"That right," Marcus answered, sounding genuinely surprised that anybody had known or cared what happened to the colony ship. "It was pretty hard times for the first generation because the Dollnick ship was beat, and everything was designed for four-armed humanoids who are also much bigger than humans. The commune couldn't put together a full ecosystem, like colony ships setting out from well-established worlds, so things kept getting out of balance and required a lot of meddling."

"What do you mean?" Chastity asked. She wasn't really that interested in colony ship operation, but she didn't want Marcus to forget that she was there.

"My father told me that they were always swinging between not enough bees and too many bees, which is no fun in a closed space," Marcus explained. "But that's just what he was interested in, personally. There were lots of missing steps in the food chain, and they ended up needing to stop and synthesize fertilizer all the time, not to mention making up water losses from interstellar ice. In the end, the commune probably wouldn't have survived if they had anything like a full complement, but there weren't even two hundred thousand people on a ship built for over a million Dollnicks, so there was plenty of room for mistakes."

"And you just happened to visit Union Station at the same time as the Wanderers?" Chastity asked.

"What gave you that idea?" Marcus said, turning fully to face her now. "We're as much a part of the mob as any of them. The commune voted to join when I was just a kid and the mob was visiting Kalthair Two, where we were working the asteroid belts."

"Is that all there is to it?" Clive asked. "If you come across a Wanderer mob and you have a colony ship or some other space-worthy environment, you can join up?"

"Sure," Marcus said. "You don't even need a ship of your own. Just an invitation," he added suggestively, not taking his eyes off of Chastity.

"But how do you make a living with your mining operation if you spend all of your time traveling with the Wanderers?" Blythe asked. "There don't seem to be any factory ships in the mob, and a friend of mine who's been visiting the larger habitats in her capacity as our cultural attaché reports that most of the farming and food production is handled by mechanicals and automated systems."

"That's right," Marcus replied proudly. "The commune had to upgrade the Intrepid's systems before joining up for just that reason. The Wanderers said that if we were going to spend all of our time feeding ourselves, there wasn't any point in coming. Fortunately, the commune was able to trade its mining stake to some sort of AI hive in return for retooling the ship."

"So what do you do when you're not dancing?" Chastity said in a teasing voice, lifting one of his wrists as she spoke. "I take you for the professional type. Maybe a scientist or a lawyer?"

"Are you trying to curse me?" Marcus laughed nervously and made a motion like he was throwing salt over his shoulder. "I'm not even thirty yet, much less forty. What would I want with such tedious hobbies at my age? Come on," he said, rising from his chair and fluidly pulling Chastity after him, as if the whole maneuver was a rehearsed dance move. "The band is coming back out and I want to get a space in the first rotation."

Chastity cast a look of puzzlement back at her sister, who merely raised an eyebrow and mouthed the word, "Bum." Then she let Marcus sweep her off in a series of dips and twirls, just his way of warming up before the music started.

"Well, that pretty much agrees with what we've been hearing from Lynx and the trainees that Joe and Woojin have been running back and forth to give them a little taste of field work," Clive commented. "It seems that the Wanderers have developed a post-employment society, and most of them don't work at anything at all."

"It doesn't make any sense," Blythe objected. "I never would have believed it if we hadn't been here ourselves, but Marcus basically told us that all he does is play."

"He's pretty good at it," Clive observed. "I suppose that even though the mob includes humans and some other backwards species, taken as a whole, they'd qualify as an advanced society, and automation has replaced the need for most labor."

"But what's the point of getting up in the morning, of raising a family, if all you're going to do is live off of the labor of mechanicals and the technology of previous generations?" Blythe asked, more perplexed than angry. "It's like they're on some sort of perpetual party-cruise, and nobody ever presents a bill!"

"You knew what to expect before we came," Clive reminded her. "Tinka said that the Drazens consider the Wanderers to be a benign parasite, a dumping ground for individuals who just don't want to work. But still, you'd think they'd need to produce something in order to keep their mob going. The drone ships that Stryx Dreel gave them to create temporary tunnels are self-maintaining, but the colony ships we passed during the taxi ride all look like cast-offs and obsolete models that must require regular investments for upkeep. I wonder where the money comes from?"

"Maybe it's like a cult and the new members who join have to give up all of their assets," Blythe suggested. "The story Marcus told, where the commune had to give up the mining claim they developed to overhaul the Intrepid before they joined? Maybe that covered repairs for some of the mob as well."

"I guess we can ask him when they get back. He didn't seem particularly secretive about anything."

"Still, you'd think they'd have to get money from somewhere," Blythe speculated, drawn in by the puzzle. "I guess they're making some good creds off of the Union Station tourist trade right now, at least, the taxi drivers and the bartenders are doing well. But where does Marcus get the money to eat and drink, or is that free as a birthright on his own ship?

"We'll just have to get the answers the old-fashioned way," Clive answered with a smile. "By spying, assuming that Chastity isn't interrogating young Marcus as we speak."

"There's something funny about the whole setup," Blythe said, standing up. "Especially the way the other species and the Stryx regard the Wanderers as a mere nuisance. It can't just be that they know how to have a good time. Come on, now. We haven't danced in ages."

"I can't do this tango thing," Clive replied, remaining in his seat. "I'd step on your feet and then I'd sprain my bad knee trying to do one of those lunge moves."

"We'll move over a couple sections," Blythe said. "There's something like a waltz starting in about five minutes, according to the map. All I ask is that you hold my waist, my hand, and pretend to lead."

Five

"Isn't this a bit over the top for a potluck reception?" Lynx asked, as she helped Kelly push the food trolley from the docking bay towards the lift tube of the Wanderer flagship. The vessel was the size of a small moon, though cylindrical like Union Station, and the internal layout bore a surprising resemblance to the standardized Stryx station, albeit on a much smaller scale. "I would have thought that the keg and the case of wine were more than sufficient." She gestured with her head at the two men who walked ahead of them, Joe guiding a keg on a hand truck, and Woojin carrying a full case of wine.

"I asked Bork for advice, and he told me to bring as much as we could manage, so maybe he's counting on us to cover for the Drazens as well," Kelly replied. "It's the first bring-your-own diplomatic event I've ever attended, but everybody says the Wanderers do things differently." She shot Lynx a sidelong glance. "How about you? Are you all rested up after your big night?"

"I slept eleven hours," Lynx replied with a groan. "I might not have made it if Wooj hadn't called last night and offered to come by and help. How can two-year-olds be so relentless? Does Blythe make them nap all day to prepare for the sitter?"

"I should have loaned you Beowulf," Kelly said. "He used to be uncomfortable around small children, but since he came back, he seems to prefer their company to us old folks. He can spend hours herding the twins, and they can spend hours trying to get away from him. It's really kind of fun watching them play together."

"Come on, I think we'll all just fit." Joe beckoned them from the lift tube capsule, where he propped the hand-truck with the keg in the corner and Woojin set the case of wine on the capsule floor. "Just push it in towards the other corner there, and I think the door will close."

The four humans and their improvised catering operation did just fit into the capsule, and Kelly told the lift, "Envoy's reception." Nothing happened.

"What's wrong with the lift?" Lynx asked. "Do you think we're over capacity or something?"

"Maybe it doesn't understand English," Joe suggested, and tried repeating the request in a few of the languages he'd picked up in his mercenary days.

"Envoy's reception, please," Kelly tried again, wondering if they had hurt the feelings of whatever AI handled the Wanderer ship's infrastructure by omitting the magic word in their prior attempts.

"That will be fourteen creds," a neutral voice told them. A panel next to the door slid aside, revealing something like a Stryx mini-register.

"They're charging us to attend their reception?" Kelly asked incredulously.

"Are you addressing me?" the voice responded.

"Uh, yes, sort-of," Kelly replied. "We represent the EarthCent embassy on Union Station, and we were invited to the official arrival reception on this ship. It seems, well, odd, that our hosts would charge us for attending."

"I can't speak for the biologicals, I'm just a working lift tube," the voice replied plaintively. "Do you think power and maintenance are free? Would you prefer transportation with components operating beyond their design life? Will fourteen creds make that much difference to your embassy's budget?"

Kelly was struck dumb by the depressed-sounding AI and its litany of complaints. She looked to Joe, who shrugged, and began fishing in his pocket for his programmable cred.

"How about five creds in untraceable cash?" Lynx inquired.

"That will be fine," the voice responded, suddenly chipper. Lynx inserted a five-cred coin in the slot. "Next stop, Envoy's reception. Keep a hand on your change purse and don't invite anybody home with you," the lift tube advised in a friendly manner.

In less than a minute, the capsule arrived at its destination and the EarthCent delegation emerged into a cavernous hall that could easily hold thousands of humanoids, though it was only half full at the moment. Hundreds of round tables with cheap plastic tablecloths were peopled with gaudily dressed members of at least two dozen species. Kelly was immediately struck by the lack of an official greeting line, but before she could plan their next move, Joe nudged her and pointed.

"Look there," he said, indicating an overdressed Frunge followed by twenty or more liveried serving men. The Frunge turned his head to acknowledge the greetings of a table full of his compatriots, and Kelly saw to her surprise that it was Czeros. Even more shocking, he appeared to be stone sober, steady on his feet and nary a tremor in his hair vines.

"And there's Acria," Lynx said, pointing out the current Vergallian ambassador, who was circulating with a whole

43

train of wait staff she must have borrowed from a banquet hall on the Vergallian deck. All of a sudden, the food trolley that Lynx had thought was overkill began to look like a diplomatic faux pas.

"This looks less like bring-your-own than bring enough for everybody else," Woojin commented. "I wonder why the advanced species all go along with it."

"You're blocking the path," rumbled a deep voice, and the humans quickly turned to see the Verlock ambassador making his way into the hall. Behind him came a whole phalanx of serving bots from the Verlock embassy, bearing what appeared to be the entire contents of a well-stocked cafeteria. Ambassador Srythlan, with whom Kelly had formed a cordial relationship, inched by the humans, as his much faster serving bots spread out among the Verlock tables.

"Ambassador," Kelly addressed him. "Could you spare a minute? It seems to me that I may have misunderstood the invitation. Are the invited diplomats supposed to bring enough food for all of these people?"

"The Verlocks have a saying," the ambassador replied like molasses, maintaining his slow progress into the hall. "Feed the mob elders or your home world will feed the entire mob."

"Hold on a minute, everybody," Kelly said, ushering the little knot of humans further to the side. "Libby?" she subvoced. "Can you hear me?"

"Certainly," the Stryx librarian replied over her diplomatic implant. "Is there a problem at the reception?"

"I don't think we brought enough," Kelly said. "I don't really understand what's going on here, but I certainly don't want to be responsible for this mob showing up at Earth!"

44

"Don't worry," Libby reassured her. "The Wanderers won't visit a Stryx protectorate without permission. It's the Naturals League members who have to tread lightly. Besides, you're only expected to supply the elders of your own species, and there may not even be any at the reception."

"Thanks, Libby," Kelly replied, and turned back to her companions. "We're off the hook on the Verlock saying. It doesn't apply to sentients in the remedial program."

"I've been doing a rough count of the tables, and it looks like a quarter of the aliens being waited on are either Horten or Drazen," Woojin said. "It's strange to see them getting along so well."

"Thick as thieves, I would say!" Bork paused to deliver this judgment, allowing the veritable train of chefs and kitchen bots he headed to stream past, bearing steaming cauldrons of traditional Drazen soups. "We got lucky, though. There can't be more than two thousand of them here. I'm told that the elder representatives of some mobs reach into the tens of thousands."

"Why didn't you warn me?" Kelly asked. "I wouldn't have accepted the invitation."

"And cause a diplomatic incident?" Bork shook his head. "Wanderers are a nuisance, but compared to supporting a population of non-productive citizens or watching them starve, the mobs are a bargain."

"You mean the advanced species use them as a sort of a dumping ground for undesirables?" Kelly asked in an undertone.

"Not exactly," Bork answered. "Nobody is exiled to the Wanderers, but they are a natural magnet for the malcontents and layabouts, those who are less interested in raising the next generation than raising a glass. We view

45

them as a sort of a safety valve, but they've been around forever, and there are certain proprieties to observe. If you'll excuse me, I have egos to flatter."

The Drazen ambassador waded into the crush and approached the nearest table populated by his kind, where he put his acting experience to good use playing the part of a gracious host.

"There should be some humans here," Lynx said. "Chastity's friend told her that a human commune on the Intrepid colony ship joined up a couple decades ago."

"Maybe that's not enough time to rank as an elder," Kelly speculated. "The title doesn't seem to be age-related, though. Some of the guests are younger than the ambassadors and their staffs."

"There, in the back," Woojin pointed. "Looks like a single table of humans to me, though we won't know for sure until we get close."

"You're on point," Joe said. He followed with the hand truck after the ex-officer carrying the case of wine. Kelly and Lynx got the food trolley moving, and were surprised to find that they were able to thread through the crowd without difficulty.

As Woojin had pointed out earlier, the elders were heavily salted with Drazens and Hortens, but there were large numbers of Verlocks, Dollnicks and Vergallians, and even a contingent of Cherts. The only species she missed from her usual diplomatic circles were the Grenouthians and the Gem. The former were probably all too industrious to join up, and the latter had likely been excluded by anti-clone bias.

"You folks from the Intrepid commune?" Joe asked in his friendly manner, raising the hand-truck handles so the keg sat flat on the deck. "We're the EarthCent delegation. It's our first time to one of these things."

"We were beginning to wonder if anybody would come," grumped an older man, who was wearing an odd purple vest with ribbons on the chest. "Don't you realize how much it would hurt our status in the mob if nobody showed up to acknowledge our contributions?"

"This is our first encounter with Wanderers," Kelly replied, leaving Lynx to maneuver the trolley into place alongside the table. "We really don't know anything about this culture or your place in it, but I'm sure you can fill us in."

"Just as soon as you fill us up." The apparent leader of the Intrepid commune cast a hungry look at EarthCent's offerings. "It's a good thing there's just the eight of us since you only brought the one load."

"Eight of you and four of us," Lynx pointed out. "Surely you don't expect us to serve and watch you eat."

"Look around you," the old man said. "Do you see any of the alien diplomats and their staff eating? The Envoy's reception takes place after you all serve the traditional meal. Remind me to give you the envelope before I leave."

"This really isn't what I was expecting," Kelly muttered, but looking around at the other tables, it was obvious that the human elder wasn't lying. All over the hall, diplomatic delegations from Union Station were directing their support personnel in serving at the tables of their species. The ambassadors seemed to be taking it in good spirit, or perhaps they were just better actors than Kelly had realized. Czeros was entertaining a group of Frunge elders just two tables away, where he was standing on a chair and performing a song-and-pantomime routine that reminded her of "I'm a Little Teapot."

47

"When in Rome, do as Romans do," Woojin suggested, uncorking a bottle of wine. He took a white cloth napkin from the food trolley, draped it over his arm, and began pouring for the eight human elders.

"I guess he means us," Lynx said to Kelly. She began pulling out the appetizers from the cooler section. Kelly quickly went over the contents of the hot section in her head, and felt a sudden burst of gratitude towards Bork for telling her to bring all she could manage. As long as the Intrepid's elders weren't huge eaters, their supplies would suffice, and the EarthCent delegation might even be able to make a quick meal out of the leftovers.

Once Joe tapped the keg, the atmosphere at the human table lightened up remarkably. They discovered that the Intrepid commune lacked a brewing tradition of their own, and the elders meant to catch up on decades of unintentional abstinence from the beverage. The beer did its work, filling bellies and loosening lips, and soon the EarthCent caterers knew more about the elder delegation's view of themselves and the place of the Wanderers in the galaxy than they cared to.

"So let me make sure I have this straight," Kelly said to Monos, the old man in the purple vest having finally admitted to owning a name. "The Wanderers offset the negative energy created by the hard-working members of your respective species by boycotting the rat race and dedicating yourselves to a life of leisure."

"We maintain a balance in the universe," Monos confirmed. "Yin and yang. Work and play. Creation and destruction. Without the Wanderers, you kinetic types would use up all of the energy in the universe that much faster."

48

"I'm not sure that entirely makes sense to me," Kelly replied cautiously, having done her best to listen to what the elders were saying for nearly an hour. "Don't you think..." She was interrupted by a loud bell, and all around the room, thousands of chairs scraped back from tables.

"Gotta go now," Monos told her. "Nice job with dinner, for a first try anyway. Here's your envelope, don't open it until they tell you." Without further ado, the human elders brushed past the EarthCent delegation and joined the throngs exiting the hall. Kelly shook her head in disbelief.

"Plenty of leftovers," Lynx observed. "Why don't we grab a bite while we're waiting for the next act of this clown show?"

Around them, Kelly observed the other Union Station delegations hastily putting together plates of leftovers and moving to a small section of tables near the hitherto-unused podium in the corner, so she gathered her companions and followed suit. They had barely seated themselves at a table with Bork and a few of his senior staff, when a tall Sharf stepped onto the small stage and tapped on an archaic-looking microphone.

"Hello, hello?" His voice echoed through the cavernous room. "Is this thing on?"

"Yes, Envoy," somebody called back.

"It's been a hard couple of centuries," the envoy declared, launching into his speech without bothering to introduce himself. Beside Kelly, Bork groaned and looked concerned. "Our recent path through interstellar space has reminded us yet again of the vast emptiness between stars. No species found fit to seek us out and provide parts and labor, and consequently, the faith of our mob in our vital mission was tested. Tested, but not shaken." The Sharf paused significantly at this point, and Joe nudged his wife.

"Did you see where the restrooms were, Kel?"

"I think I saw one of those signs with a humanoid standing, sitting and kneeling, next to the bank of lift tubes," Kelly responded. Joe stood quietly and began navigating his way through all of the empty tables.

"Each of the ambassadors present today was given an envelope by your co-speciesists. Do you all have them with you?" The Sharf stopped again, turning his eye stalks for a moment to follow Joe's retreating back.

"Here!" the ambassadors replied in chorus, waving the envelopes over their heads.

"It does my three hearts good to see how our sacrifices are appreciated by those we left behind," the Sharf declared. "Come now, you all know what's inside the envelope. I want you to choose the amount you're authorized to pledge, and then move your fingers one tab to the right and fold over the next higher amount instead. Think about how you're compensating for all of the hard work your species have done in accumulating the wealth that allows you to make these contributions. Think about what the galaxy would be like if the Wanderers didn't exist to balance the books."

Kelly opened her envelope and stared in shock at the pledge card. The smallest tab showed a hundred thousand creds, and the largest had more zeros than she could count. She looked around at the other tables and saw that all of the ambassadors were hesitating, staring at the pledge cards. Then the Sharf delivered his winning argument in a booming voice.

"Think about the alternative!"

Kelly saw Bork flinch and jerk his fingers to the right, quickly bending up a tab that represented an amount which was probably equal to Earth's export income for a whole year. Then he carefully ripped all the other tabs off at their base. All around them the other ambassadors were doing the same, pained looks on their faces. The EarthCent ambassador couldn't hesitate any longer.

"Libby!" she subvoced urgently. "Did you say we're exempt from a Wanderer mob visiting Earth?"

"As long as you remain a protectorate," Libby replied. "Despite the rapid progress your people are making, I'd say you're safe for at least another ten generations."

"Ten generations as in my grandchildren's grandchildren's grandchildren's..."

"Yes." Libby cut her off uncharacteristically, perhaps to save her friend from an embarrassing math error.

"So I don't have to pledge the embassy's budget for the next thousand years to these extortionists?"

"No, you don't," Libby replied.

"Just checking," Kelly subvoced back, and gleefully ripped all of the tabs off of the pledge card. When the basket reached their table, she threw it in, feeling better than she had the whole evening.

"Easy come, easy go," Bork said mournfully, throwing his own pledge card over hers. "Still, they only come around the stations every few hundred years because they know the Stryx wouldn't tolerate more frequent visits. And it explains the time-delayed communication from my predecessor."

"What's that?" Kelly asked.

"Oh, there were a number of them encoded in my office calendar when I took over this job," Bork replied. "Most of them are long-dated stuff, like the one that auto-decrypted before the ice harvesting conference a few years ago advising me to vote in favor. The one that opened up when the Wanderer fleet began arriving instructed me to pay whatever it takes, and that the home office would reimburse without arguing."

"From what I've seen of their taxi service and lift tubes, it's surprising they need to beg," Lynx muttered darkly.

"I just don't get their philosophy," Kelly said in frustration. "Why would they want to fritter away their whole lives at a non-stop party?"

Joe returned looking flushed and annoyed. "Sorry to interrupt, Kelly, but does anybody have a spare cred for the restroom door? It requires exact change."

Six

"And stretch, and two, and three, and four. And reach, and two, and three, and four." Aisha paused, a comically serious look on her face as she regarded the line of children who were all on their best behavior for the famous host of Let's Make Friends. "Now, to your marks. Let's shake it down!" she ordered, and all of the little sentients began vigorously waggling their extremities.

A Drazen boy's tentacle had almost put out a Horten girl's eye in the first season, leading Aisha to introduce the "marks" on the studio floor that showed each species where to stand. Paul had done the math on how much clearance they all needed for their various appendages, and there hadn't been any accidents for the last two years. The Grenouthians had long since perfected real-time language dubbing for holo-cast viewers without implants, and the children on the show were all equipped with an in-ear plug which received a continuous feed in their native tongue.

"Commercial!" the Grenouthian director called, on hearing which, the children all collapsed dramatically to the floor.

"Stop exaggerating," Aisha pleaded. "It's just a little exercise, and the show is already halfway over. Besides, I'll bet you've all been doing the stretches along with holo-casts in your homes."

"I only fell down because he did!" Samuel piped up, pointing at the large Dollnick child.

"Me too," chorused a number of little aliens.

"But I'm tired," the Dollnick complained tearfully. "I didn't know it would be after my bedtime."

"Didn't your parents make sure you napped today?" Aisha asked with concern.

The Dollnick child shrugged, a confusing gesture from a creature with two sets of arms.

Coordinating time schedules had always been a challenge given the show's rotation of child actors, especially since all of the aliens artificially maintained different length days on their decks. Once, Aisha had asked Paul to calculate how often they could produce a show that fell during daytime hours for all of the possible combinations of species on the station. After consulting with Jeeves, Paul told her, "Twice, if you live to a healthy old age."

So Aisha had decided to stick with the human clock, and requested that parents prepare their children to live on a different schedule for the length of their rotation on the show. The Dollnick children required daily exposure to a sequence of varying wavelengths from their artificial deck lighting to trigger the sleeping cycle, so they had trouble changing schedules. Paul explained it had to do with simulating the binary star system of their home world.

"Live in ten, nine, eight," the Grenouthian director shouted, then shifted to counting down silently, with exaggerated mouth movements that always made Aisha think of a bunny trying to ingest an enormous invisible carrot. The children clambered to their feet and gathered around the curtained pedestal for this week's surprise. In addition to exercise routines, story time, and of course, the namesake "Let's Make Friends," segment, each show included a special event that only came up once per rotation.

Some of these, like "The Ice Cream Field Trip," and "My Favorite Place," were pre-recorded and inserted into the live broadcast, which the vast majority of the audience watched on-demand. But the "Surprise" segment was always done live, and none of the actors, including Aisha, knew what would be revealed behind the curtain. Previous surprises ranged from Samuel's grandmother, who had conspired with the Grenouthians in return for a free trip, to a stable miniature black hole, fulfilling a young Verlock's request to the Volcano Creature, the Santa Claus of the mathematically oriented species.

"It's Surprise Day, and we're all waiting to see what's behind the curtain," Aisha announced after the Grenouthian finished his countdown. "Shall I pull the cord and lift the curtain?"

As always, one of the little aliens got scared and grabbed her hand. Today it was a stunning Vergallian girl, who was appearing on the show for the first time.

"What if it's the Void Man?" Ailia asked in trepidation, her eyes wide with childish fear and excitement.

"Then we'll feed him milk and cookies, and make him promise not to bother any more good children," Aisha reassured her. The girl let go, and the host of LMF pulled open the curtains, revealing a shimmering black bag that looked like it contained at least a month's worth of somebody's dirty laundry.

"Does anybody know what this is?" she asked the children.

"It's a Jort sack," the Horten boy declared confidently. "Just yank on the ribbon and it will open itself."

Aisha reached out and pulled the black ribbon tied around the neck of the sack, and the shimmering fabric seemed to dissolve. A large number of translucent polyhedrons, made visible through the light they refracted, tumbled off the pedestal and onto the stage. Freed of the high-tech packing material, a delicate statuette constructed from spun golden threads appeared. It depicted a figure in a Hindu dance posture, standing on one leg with the other leg extended before her, bent at the knee. The statuette's hands were held flat above the extended leg, one with the fingers all pointing up, the other with the fingers pointing down, as if she was trying to create a hand shadow of a bird.

"Look, children. I think it's supposed to be me!" Aisha exclaimed. Then a shot rang out, and she jumped out of her slippers.

"Bang!" Samuel shouted, and in imitation of the Horten boy, jumped on one of the packing polyhedrons with both feet. The result was an even louder explosion than the Horten had managed.

"Bang! Bang!" the alien children yelled in delight, chasing down the barely visible polyhedrons, which were as flexible as balloons, but burst with a vengeance when distorted beyond their modulus of elasticity. Even the over-tired Dollnick was revived by the game, swatting at the shapes with all four hands when they kicked up from the floor.

"Children, children," Aisha called, plainly rattled by the popping of the packing material. "Wouldn't it be more fun to gather up all of these shapes and make something with them?"

"No!" cried the Horten boy, stamping on a polyhedron with relish.

"No!" the other kids chorused, jumping here and there, creating tremendous bangs.

The little Vergallian girl shyly approached Aisha and handed her one of the light-as-air shapes.

"I'd rather make something nice, but the boys are going to pop them all," Ailia said.

"Would you like to pop this one?" the human host asked with sudden insight. The little Vergallian shook her head, first side-to-side, and then up-and-down. "Go ahead, then," Aisha said with a sigh, patting the girl's golden curls. Ailia gravely placed the shape at her feet, and then stamped on it rather tentatively, with one foot. It made a loud "pop" and she screamed happily, grabbing Aisha's hand in fright at her own daring.

It took almost five minutes for the children to finish chasing down and popping all of the polyhedrons, which was all of the time allotted for the special surprise segment of the show. The director called, "Commercial!" and the children all dove to the floor again. This time they really might have been exhausted.

"Well, I guess nobody who wants their art featured on the show will send it in that packing material again," Aisha commented to the director.

"I gave the statue a couple of long close-ups, just to break up the action," the Grenouthian replied. Although he was relatively young to be director of such an important source of revenue on the education network, the bunny was a maestro of live holo-casts, and he had been with Aisha since the beginning. "I hear your mother-in-law is going to submit a proposal."

"Yes, she co-authored the initial treatment for this show with me, you know," Aisha replied. She was now an old hand at entertainment terminology. "I want to help her, but I don't seem to be tuned in to the same wave-length as the grown-up demographic."

"No. You're kidding!" the Grenouthian said facetiously. Then he snapped to attention and began another count-in. "Live in ten, nine, eight..." The children struggled back to their feet and tried to look cute.

"I hope we used up all of our extra physical energy, because now it's time to exercise our imaginations," Aisha said. She gestured with both hands for the children to gather around. "Some of you are in your first rotation on our show, so you may not know how to play Storytellers."

"We know, we know," the children all yelled, which wasn't surprising since it was one of the most controversial and talked about segments of Let's Make Friends. Some of the straight-laced species thought it bordered on teaching children how to lie, but Aisha was adamant that imaginative storytelling was an important part of childhood development. The deciding factor was the Grenouthian analytics, which showed that the sponsors paid the most for the commercial spots before and after the storytelling.

"Today, we're going to tell a story about the Wanderers coming to visit Union Station," Aisha continued, skipping the long version of the instructions. "You may be too young to know anything about real Wanderers, so when your turn comes, just make something up!"

"I visited them!" Samuel interrupted. The other children looked at him enviously.

"I'll just begin, then," Aisha said. "Once upon..."

"A TIME!" the children shouted.

"A group of clever children from Union Station went to visit the Wanderers." Aisha stopped there and pointed at the Dollnick boy, hoping to get his contribution before he nodded off.

"The Wanderers asked the children for their money, but the Dollnick boy was a big hero and he hit them!" the Dolly child declared, shaking all of his fists in a five-year-old's fearsome display of aggression.

"Oh, dear," Aisha said. "That's not very friendly. What happened next?" she asked, pointing to Samuel.

"And then the Wanderers put all of the children into sacks, and left them in the forest near the gingerbread house," Samuel said, borrowing heavily from one of the scary picture books Dorothy had read to him.

"That's not very friendly either," Aisha said, shaking her head mournfully. The story was hardly going as she planned, and she was beginning to expect she'd be hearing from some angry Wanderers when it was over. "Didn't anything nice happen?" she asked, pointing to Ailia hopefully.

"The children's parents came looking for them, and the Wanderers told the parents where the sacks were for just ten creds each?" the Vergallian girl suggested.

"Well, I guess that's better," Aisha said, and pointed to the little Frunge.

"But when the parents found the sacks, they were all empty, and the Wanderers kept the children and the money," the Frunge contributed.

"For a whole day, before sending them home?" Aisha prompted, hoping to steer the story back towards a happy ending. She pointed to the Horten boy.

"Forever after," the Horten boy concluded. "They made the children pick up their dirty clothes and eat their blue vegetables, too!" All the kids shuddered at the horrible outcome.

"Where's Naina?" Aisha asked, looking around for the little Chert girl who tended to disappear when the going got rough. "It's your turn, Naina. If the story is too scary, you can change the ending," the host added hopefully.

"Mommy says to hide when there are Wanderers around," proclaimed a disembodied little voice. "They steal children!"

"And what do you think happened to the children in the end?" Aisha asked the Verlock child. She'd been saving him for last, because the young Verlocks were too conservative in their imaginings and tended to put an early damper on stories.

"I don't know," the Verlock said. "Maybe the Wanderers ate them up?"

The blue strobe in the studio began to flash, informing Aisha that the show had just another thirty seconds to run. She quickly found her mark and addressed the audience.

"I hope today's story doesn't keep any of you out there in holo-land from sleeping tonight," Aisha said. "But the important thing is to use your imagination, even if it sometimes takes you to scary places. Just remember that the things you imagine aren't real, and with family and friends, you don't have to face the dark alone."

The fifteen-second reel of the show's theme music began, and the children, who had gathered around Aisha as she spoke, began to sing along in their native tongues. It had taken the help of Libby to come up with a little song that rhymed in so many languages and still made sense, though the meaning varied with the species due to anatomical and cultural differences.

Don't be a stranger because I look funny,
You look weird to me, but let's make friends.
I'll give you a tissue if your nose is runny,
I'm as scared as you, so let's make friends.

60

"That's a wrap!" the director announced. "Good show, kids. Loved the story."

The children's parents swept down on stage and gathered up their suddenly exhausted offspring, the Dollnick's father cradling the boy in his arms like a sack of grain. Joe usually accompanied Samuel to the studio when the boy was in the show's rotating cast, but Kelly had brought him today to refresh her memory on Grenouthian production techniques.

"How do you time it all so closely?" Kelly asked her daughter-in-law, who had slumped into a folding chair.

"Just practice, I guess," Aisha replied wearily. "Do you think the Wanderers will be really angry about that story? It's a good thing I don't work for EarthCent anymore, or I might have triggered a diplomatic crisis."

"The Wanderers have thicker skins than the Verlocks," Kelly assured her. "Besides, they'll probably take the whole thing as a compliment on their standing. I'm sure I told you about that extortionate dinner reception."

"They can't be as bad as everybody makes them out to be," Aisha protested, with a spark of renewed energy. "I should invite their children on the show to make friends."

Kelly was still trying to come up with a response that would discourage Aisha from the experiment without awakening her stubborn streak, when Samuel ran into her legs while yelling, "Stop following me," over his shoulder.

"I just want to be friends," the angelic little Vergallian girl said tearfully. "Tell him to be friends with me," she pleaded with Aisha.

"You can't tell people to be friends," Aisha said, lifting Ailia onto her lap.

61

"Daddy says that Vergallian women are scary!" Samuel proclaimed, holding onto Kelly's legs.

"I'm not a woman, I'm a little girl," Ailia protested, to no avail.

"Where are your parents?" Aisha asked. "Didn't they come to see your first show?"

"Nurse brought me, but she had to get back to work," Ailia said. "She told me to wait here for her. We're in exile." The girl offered this explanation hesitantly, as if she was ashamed or unclear what it really meant.

"Oh," Kelly said, giving Aisha a significant look. "Maybe you should show her around the studio, Sammy, since it's her first time. I'm sure Daddy was talking about some different Vergallians."

Samuel looked doubtful, but Aisha put Ailia back on the floor and gave him an encouraging nod, so he sighed in exaggerated fashion and tried his best to look world-weary. "Come on," he said to Ailia. "Mommy wants to talk with Aunty Aisha in secret."

"Thank you," Aisha said. The two children moved off, Ailia trying to put her feet in the exact places Samuel had stepped as she followed him. "The girl seemed a bit needy during the show. I couldn't get her to let go of my hand for the first fifteen minutes, but we never found Vergallian parents willing to let their children mix with other species at this age before."

"It sounds like her family is involved in one of those endless wars of succession the Vergallian royals are always fighting," Kelly explained. "Joe and Woojin could tell you about them, and Clive has probably fought in them too, for that matter. They use lots of mercenaries, and since the wars only end when one family is wiped out, parents often send their youngest daughter away in case of defeat."

Kelly paused and looked around to make sure the children weren't in hearing distance. "If this girl's guardian has to work to support them, I'd guess her family lost."

"Oh, no!" Aisha cried. "I'll wait with her and talk to the nurse when she comes. Won't the other Vergallians on the station help her?"

"Not unless she's related," Kelly said. "You can tell just by looking at her that she's from the ruling class, so the commoners won't have anything to do with her, and with no family, the upper class will shun her. Joe always said that the Vergallians are a hard people, though Clive claims that one saved his life."

"Kelly?" Libby asked over the ambassador's implant. "Do you mind if I speak to you and Aisha at the same time?"

"No, that's fine, Libby," Kelly answered out loud. It was the first time she could recall the station librarian asking this question, and she wondered what it was all about. Apparently, Aisha also answered in the affirmative, because Libby continued.

"It's about the Vergallian girl," Libby said sadly. "I was listening in to your conversation because, well, I always listen in if you don't tell me otherwise. I cross-referenced the girl's story against our records to see where her nurse is working. It turns out she left the station twenty minutes ago on a Vergallian space liner, and they've already gone through the tunnel."

"She abandoned Ailia?" Aisha asked in shock, not thinking to subvoc. Fortunately, the children were still at the other side of the stage, where Samuel was now trying to stop the girl from following in his exact footsteps, though his mother could tell that he actually enjoyed the attention.

"I'm afraid Kelly's speculation about the girl's family was correct," Libby continued. "Either they failed to arrange for continued payments to the nurse after their demise, or, more likely, the nurse was a trusted retainer who simply took the first opportunity to abandon her charge. I could investigate further, but I don't see the use."

"Can you contact the Vergallian ambassador?" Aisha asked Kelly. "Maybe she'll help."

"I doubt that very much," Libby interjected. "In any case, the Vergallians are swapping again. The latest ambassador is gone and I don't expect the new one until next week."

"Is there any way to find her a temporary home with the Vergallians on the station?" Kelly asked Libby.

"You might find some commoners willing to take her in for a substantial fee, but she would be ostracized by everybody around her," Libby said. "It would be better to put her in our orphanage, where at least she would get a good education."

"I'm keeping her for the time being," Aisha declared. "We'll just tell her that her nurse got called away for an emergency."

Samuel returned, jumping from one foot to the next in huge steps, an impressive display of coordination for a five-year-old. All of the yoga exercises and the occasional dance lessons were paying off. Ailia did her best to dog his moves, but she lost her balance at the last leap and staggered into the arms of Aisha, who had quickly crouched to catch her.

"Your nurse was called away on an emergency, so you're coming home with us," Aisha told the girl, holding her gently and looking directly into her eyes. "Okay?"

"Nurse isn't coming back," Ailia said sadly, trying to blink away tears. "Nobody ever comes back." She didn't stop crying until she fell asleep in the Vergallian-style hammock that Paul quickly improvised for her in their bedroom on the ice harvester in Mac's Bones.

Seven

"I can't tell the difference, can you?" Shaina asked Chastity. She handed over the five-cred coin Ian had given her. The owner of Pub Haggis had closed the restaurant for the afternoon to host an emergency meeting of Kelly's contacts from the Shuk, the Little Apple, and the business community. Kelly was attending in her official capacity as the EarthCent Ambassador, and she sat next to Stanley, who had taken over financial management for InstaSitter.

"It looks good to me," the co-owner of InstaSitter said. She rolled the coin between her knuckles, bit it, and then bounced it off the bar. Shaina watched these proceedings with amusement. "I saw it in an immersive once, but I guess it only works for gold," Chastity explained.

"We've been getting a couple of these a night," Ian said. The pub owner was standing on the other side of the bar where he worked drawing beers for the attendees. "Not enough to really hurt yet, but we're going to start running all of the small coins through the mini-register just to verify them, and that's going to slow down every cash transaction. Most of the merchants in the Little Apple have mini-registers, of course, but it would be too big an investment for the corridor vendors and traders, so they'll probably just pass the bad creds along."

"They won't even know they're passing bad creds," Stanley pointed out.

"Are we sure the counterfeits are coming in from the Wanderer visitors?" Kelly asked.

"We had a Shuk-wide meeting last night, all species," Peter said. "First time everybody has gotten together like that since I've been on the station, so they're all taking this seriously. From what the aliens say, counterfeit coins always start turning up whenever a mob comes around, and there's no way to stop it unless you search every visitor to the station."

"So much for the Styx cred being the ultimate currency." Ian snorted disdainfully and pushed a couple of beers across the bar.

"Don't throw away the counterfeits," Peter cautioned them. "The Shuk merchants said the Stryx will make them good and settle the issue with the Wanderers directly. In the meantime, Gryph has prohibited informal taxi services from bringing Wanderers onto the station. Any new arrivals from the mob have to take the scheduled shuttles and submit to a thorough scan when they disembark."

"I heard from Libby that Gryph instituted a quota for Wanderer visitors as soon as they arrived," Kelly ventured. "I guess this explains it, though I don't understand why the Wanderers would risk getting the Stryx angry. I mean, they must know that they'd be caught and punished."

"InstaSitter doesn't accept cash payments, so the main problem for us has been that some customers are unwittingly tipping their sitters with bad coins," Stanley said. "As far as sophisticated crime goes, these counterfeiters are on about the same level as shoplifters. Duplicating the appearance of the coins isn't even advanced tech, they're just replicas."

"Sorry I'm late," Jeeves announced, floating into the room. "I wanted to pop out to the Wanderer mob for a look around before coming. It's the first opportunity I've had to see one in person."

"Did you find the counterfeiters?" Shaina asked. Four years of working with Jeeves in their auction circuit business had brought home the fact that the only limitation on the Stryx's ability to solve problems was the self-imposed rule not to interfere in the normal workings of the galactic community more than necessary.

"Was I supposed to?" Jeeves asked. "It wouldn't be so easy in any case. All they need is basic metal forming technology and a reasonable approximation of the alloy components for feed stock. It's likely that the fakes are being produced on some of the ten thousand or so small vessels that just tow along with the colony ships. It's the encryption they can't duplicate, but biologicals have no way of checking that without using tools."

"That's it?" Ian asked. "The Stryx response is that it can't be helped, but you'll exchange good creds for bad and try to collect before the mob leaves?"

"Gryph is a little more proactive than that," Jeeves said calmly. "But you have to keep this in perspective. It's a small number of low denomination fixed-value coins, not the programmable creds which account for more than ninety-nine point nine percent of the Stryx cred money supply. Besides, according to the Grenouthian documentary about Earth's old economic system, humans should view what the Wanderers are doing as a form of economic stimulus."

"Counterfeiting was supposed to be good for the economy?" Kelly asked in surprise. She turned to Stanley for confirmation, knowing he had been writing a PhD dissertation on economic game theory before he quit for a "serious" job in the gaming industry.

"When the central banks printed extra money, they called it stimulus instead of counterfeiting," Stanley said. "Of course, they had already given up on ever putting the cat back in the bag, and were engaged in a global devaluation race with negative interest rates when the Stryx stepped in and opened Earth. Towards the end, the banks were charging people to accept deposits and paying people to borrow."

"I think you've had too much to drink," Ian said, jokingly pulling away Stanley's beer. "What, were you serious?"

"Your countries all used fiat money at that period," Jeeves answered for Stanley. "For the purpose of creating economic activity, it theoretically didn't matter whether the central banks created the money or whether people printed their own at home, providing it would pass as good and they didn't get caught. In fact, one of your dissenting economists of the day argued that counterfeiting by criminal gangs was more effective at stimulating economic activity than official money creation, because the criminal counterfeits got into the hands of people who would spend it, while the central bank money just caused asset appreciation, making the rich richer."

"If that's the case, why isn't the same true with the Stryx cred?" Kelly demanded.

"Our currency isn't fiat money, it's all backed by real property," Jeeves explained. "You know that we track the flows closely through the register network, and we keep the total Stryx cred supply far below the asset base, namely station real estate. Of course, we also maintain extensive reserves of all of the extent galactic currencies, so rather than redeeming creds for a piece of a station, we can exchange into the currency or commodity of choice."

"The same as the pension funds you run for InstaSitter and EarthCent Intelligence," Chastity observed. "They're backed by the cash flow from rentals of station real estate."

"But what if everybody stopped paying rent?" Kelly asked, still trying to get a handle on the system.

"That hasn't happened as long as the tunnel network has been in existence," Jeeves replied. "But if it did, Gryph assures me that Stryx cred holders and pensioners could redeem their holdings for partial ownership in the stations, though for a variety of reasons, they would be better off accepting commodities or other currencies."

"And what prevents rich people from simply accumulating Stryx creds until they own everything?" A reflexive desire to defend Earth's history drove Kelly to play the devil's advocate. "I'd think that after tens of millions of years of everybody accepting the Stryx cred as the galaxy's most trusted currency, you'd have created far more of it than the value of the stations."

"They can't be hoarded," Stanley informed her. "Didn't you know that the programmable creds have a built in half-life that causes the value to deteriorate if the money isn't circulated?"

"We, or should I say, the first generation Stryx, created the cred to encourage interspecies economic activity," Jeeves explained. "That can only happen through trade in goods and services. The successful businessmen know that if they start accumulating Stryx creds, they have to use them or gradually lose them. The true misers, and they exist in every species, end up exchanging Stryx creds into their local currency so they can hoard that, but of course, the local currency ends up losing value versus the cred."

"It's really a slick system," Stanley added. "It doesn't prevent individuals or species from hoarding wealth, as you know. Just look at the old Kasilians or the Dollnick merchant princes. But the real effect of their hoarding is just to drive up the prices of rare artworks and artifacts that aren't part of everyday economic activity. It's not like the old days on Earth, when financial inflation made it impossible for young people to save for retirement because every investment turned into a pyramid scheme. The Stryx maintain economic growth without inflation, and the money is recycled back to them in station rents, fees for tunnel usage, ship controllers, and the various technologies they license."

"When did you learn all of this, Dad?" Chastity asked.

"The details are all in the End User License Agreement for the InstaSitter Stryx cred register," Stanley replied.

"So are we going to do something about the Wanderers or not?" Ian demanded. The pub owner had a particular grudge against the bad coins, because he had only found out he was accepting them when the counter kid at the local coffee shop had refused to take a five-cred piece that Ian proffered to pay for his drink. Ian was up for reelection as the president of the Little Apple council of merchants, and getting accused of passing bad coins didn't fit in with his campaign.

"You shouldn't talk about them like they're all crooks," Chastity protested. "It's not like we don't have any con artists and rogue traders here on the station."

"I heard somebody has been visiting Dance Hall every night," Jeeves commented.

"Don't you start in on me," Chastity warned the Stryx. "I'm in agreement with Chance that there's nothing worse than robot gossips."

"Even though the Wanderer visitors are mainly from the same species as the merchants on the Shuk deck, they often give themselves away," the Hadad patriarch said, in an effort to steer the conversation back on track. "Sometimes they forget that they're shopping and they ask if they can have whatever it is gratis."

"They walk up to a booth and request free goods?" Ian asked in astonishment. "Maybe they aren't crooks after all. Maybe they're just nuts."

"They do seem to live by a different set of rules," Kelly said. "And the important thing to remember here is that all of the advanced species are willing to put up with them, at least to a point. I think they see the Wanderers as a sort of safety valve for the misfits from their own societies."

"The Wanderers have their part to play," Jeeves said agreeably. "Among other things, despite the negative connotation certain people attach to gossiping, the Wanderers are an excellent source for information on progress around the galaxy. They go everywhere, get into everything, and even take samples of populations with them when they leave."

"So visiting them is like doing field research by looking in a vacuum cleaner," Shaina hazarded a comparison.

"Now you're calling the Wanderers garbage!" Chastity bristled, getting really upset. "You have to put yourselves in their shoes to understand where they're coming from. At first glance, they seem to be a mix of parasites and hustlers, but if you take the time to get to know them..."

"They turn out to be really good dancers?" Stanley interrupted.

Chastity glared at her father and then sank back into her chair, muttering to herself. Jeeves floated over to the bar and began examining the jar of counterfeit creds that Ian had collected. The Stryx studied the coins one by one, moving so rapidly that the humans all stopped what they were doing to watch the blur of his pincer. Four narrow towers of coins seemed to grow out of the bar, and a few shorter stacks were placed around them, like an architect's conception of a multi-purpose complex.

"There you have it," Jeeves declared. "Your sample includes counterfeits from thirteen different replication processes, likely run by different Wanderer families or groups. The composition of the feed alloys varies more than one would expect, so there's probably not much cooperation among the counterfeiters. Perhaps they are from different species as well."

"And that's just based on my sample," Ian said thoughtfully. "We mainly get humans in here, a few Drazen, the occasional Frunge, Vergallian or Horten. Maybe the heights of the stacks correlate in some way with our customer base."

"A good guess," Jeeves acknowledged. "Gryph is waiting for the situation to stabilize before buying in the counterfeits, so these are the only samples I've examined. But the records from prior Wanderer visits indicate a sort of affinity network. The counterfeiters are most comfortable spending the coins they manufacture with their own species."

"You really go through this every time the Wanderers visit?" Kelly asked. "Why didn't Gryph start with the tight visitor controls when the mob first showed up if he knew this was going to happen?"

"Punishing the children for the sins of their fathers?" the older Hadad asked. "Besides, it makes sense that the Stryx can't get worked up over something they see on a regular basis and view as a minor nuisance. But you should probably send a warning to Earth in case the Wanderers pay a visit. It wouldn't take too many bad creds

73

to have a real impact on the economy there, and who knows if the Stryx would make good."

"We wouldn't," Jeeves answered the unasked question. "It would be too tempting for humans to start counterfeiting creds on their own and blaming it on the visitors."

"The Wanderers are proscribed from visiting Earth until the Stryx let us out from under their wings, so it won't be a problem for a long time," Kelly added.

"Does anybody on the station try counterfeiting creds and passing them off as being imported by the Wanderers?" Shaina asked Jeeves out of curiosity.

"Not according to the records," the Stryx replied instantly. "The risk is high and the reward is low, so it wouldn't make much sense. There are frequently cases of traders from various species rushing to a station that the Wanderers are visiting to exchange bad coins passed to them elsewhere. Gryph's policy is to analyze the coins and exchange any which were manufactured by the mob currently visiting the station. It's not generally worth the expenses of the trip unless the trader has accumulated a large number of counterfeits or knows ahead of time which Wanderer mob made them."

"Well, I have to get back to the embassy to work on my pilot show," Kelly said, bringing the informal meeting to a conclusion. "It's not too late to drop in and give me suggestions if you have any. We're currently planning a quiz show where contestants from all of the species ask each other questions, rather than the host asking them."

"That could prove interesting," Jeeves commented.

Eight

"Actually, I'm the EarthCent Cultural Attaché on Union Station," Lynx told the Wanderer storyteller group. "Whoever gave you the idea I was an agent?"

"He did," replied the wrinkled old Drazen woman sitting at the head of the table, pointing a bony finger at Thomas. "He said that the two of you were EarthCent Intelligence agents. We wouldn't have agreed to talk with just anybody."

"Oh, that's what you meant," Lynx said, putting her improvisation skills to work. "My translation implant must have glitched. I thought you asked if I was a talent agent who could represent you. Of course we're spies. Thomas and I were the first two agents they hired when the agency was started."

The Drazen studied her skeptically, but decided to let it pass. The eldest human storyteller from the mob present, Monos, was harder to convince.

"If you're really a spy, do something spy-like," he demanded in a crotchety tone.

"Yeah, let's see some secret weapons," said a Drazen male, who looked almost as old as the head elder of the group.

"I didn't bring anything with me," Lynx protested, drawing a Bronx cheer from the human. "Do you have any spy stuff today, Thomas?"

"Put an apple on your head." Thomas slid his partner the fruit basket and then walked around to the far side of the table. Several of the dozing elders came back to life at this directive, and began to nudge each other with creaky elbows and withered tentacles. Shooting a piece of fruit off of somebody's head was a foundational myth for many species, but none of the sentients present had ever seen it acted out before.

"I'm not putting an apple on my head!" Lynx tried to make her objection sound final. "Besides, you don't have a bow and arrow."

"I've been training with Woojin," Thomas said. "I now know sixty-three ways to kill a man with common household items. What's the matter? Are you afraid you can't keep an apple balanced?"

"I'm afraid you're going to put my eye out with a common household item," she retorted, doing a quick inventory of the table for dangerous weapons.

"No apple, no stories," the old Drazen woman stated flatly.

"Don't worry, partner," Thomas reassured her, feeling around inside his immaculately tailored suit coat. "I almost never miss in practice."

"No knives or forks," Lynx stipulated, rummaging through the fruit for an apple with a nice concave bottom. She wondered whose stupid idea it had been to bring the fruit basket, and then realized Thomas had suggested it. Clearly, she had been set up.

The old folks were becoming restless as Lynx stalled for time, examining each piece of fruit, and Monos began making "Brawk, brawk," noises, implying that she was chicken. Annoyed at everyone and everything, she settled on an apple at random, stood back from the table, and placed it on her head.

"Do you want me to warn you before I throw?" Thomas asked.

"Yes," Lynx hissed between clenched teeth, trying to speak without moving her jaw. "If you hit me, I'm going to..."

Before she could finish her threat, her partner's hand flashed forward, and although she didn't feel the impact, she heard a small noise. The apple rolled from her head, bounced off her shoulder, and hit the floor.

"The apple doesn't fall far from the tree," the old human remarked with a snicker.

Lynx bent to retrieve the bruised piece of fruit. A pencil had speared it right through the core and protruded out the other side, though thanks to the fall, the point had broken off. Seeing the penetration, she realized that Thomas must have thrown the light pencil really hard.

"There, do you accept that I'm a spy now?" she demanded, placing the apple in front of the Drazen crone. The old heads around the table all nodded.

"We would have believed you if you had just showed us the pencil," the old Drazen male said. "Who but a spy would carry such a thing?"

"I brought extras, in case anybody else wants to stand with an apple," Thomas offered.

"Perhaps another time," the eldest answered with alacrity. "Now, remind me again why you wanted to see us."

Lynx groaned internally. Here they were on a mission to gather intelligence through the rumors passed along by storytellers, and their potential source couldn't remember something from yesterday. Fortunately, Thomas had no problem with recapping his previous encounter with the chief storyteller.

"We met in Dance Hall where you were telling a story during a band break," Thomas reminded her. "I approached you and asked if you had any stories about dangerous goings-on, and you said that the Wanderers didn't want to hear those. So I said that I was a spy and I'd like to hear them, but I wanted to bring my partner if I could, and you said that was fine because you were tired anyway. Then I bought you a fancy pink drink that bubbled so much that I got little drops on my suit sleeve, which bleached the fabric white, and you said if you were a hundred years younger, you'd show me how to really tango. Then I..."

"That's enough, Thomas," the Drazen woman interrupted, and smiled. "If you go on any longer, I'll forget the beginning, but you show an excellent aptitude for story-telling."

"Do you want to hear about the time Lynx and I photographed a Horten superstar on a Farling world?" Thomas asked.

"Please, Thomas," Lynx interjected. "We're here on a spy mission, remember?" She invoked one of the mantras of EarthCent Intelligence's spy camp. "We listen with our ears, not with our mouths."

"Would you like to hear about dangerous events from long ago, or from our recent travels?" the old Drazen woman asked.

"Recent travels," Lynx replied instantly, to prevent Thomas from saying the opposite. The artificial person had developed a fascination with history, perhaps because his own was so limited.

"I am oldest, so I shall begin," the old woman declared in a formal manner. The other storytellers sat back in their chairs, closing their eyes in concentration or drowsiness. "A few years ago, our mob was recovering satellites from orbit around Gnosis Five, a former Dollnick ag world whose sun had grown unstable."

"So the satellites were salvage?" Lynx asked.

"That's exactly what we said, but a group of Dollnick farmers living there accused us of disrupting their weather control network," the storyteller replied. "In any case, they threatened to target us with their anti-asteroid defenses, which we pointed out is a clear breach of the license agreement for planetary protection systems funded through Stryx grants."

"I didn't realize the Dollnicks accepted hand-outs like that from the Stryx," Lynx said.

"They don't, but we were trying to buy time to recover at least one full quadrant of the grid," the old Drazen woman explained. "The resale value for orphan weather control satellites is terrible. You basically need to find a world running an identical system in need of spares."

"I'm not sure I understand this story," Thomas said slowly. "You were stealing..."

"Harvesting," the Drazen male interrupted the artificial person.

"You were harvesting satellites from an active weather control system and the owners objected?"

"Correct," the elder said, and resumed her narrative. "They weren't having any of it, apparently they had dealt with a mob before, and they sent a couple asteroid-busters across the bow of our flagship to make their point. Well, we issued the recall for all of the shuttles and tugs chasing down satellites, and offered the Dollys a very good price for restoring the previously harvested satellites to their stations."

"Ransom," Lynx interpreted.

"Finder's fees. So they made a big deal over the price, which you expect from Dollnicks, and then proposed to target us on general principle. The Sharf who runs our mob pointed out that destroying us wouldn't do anything for their weather, which was deteriorating rapidly. So we came to an arrangement, but they absolutely refused to let us send any of our people down, including our Dollnicks. They also said if they saw us back again, they were going to shoot first and ask questions later."

"Seems pretty reasonable of them," Thomas commented.

"Yes, we thought so also," the Drazen woman concluded, and bit into a pear. "These are really good. You grow them on the station?"

"That's it?" Lynx said. "I ask for a story about galactic dangers and you tell me about your mob extorting ransom money from a failing Dollnick ag world?"

"They didn't have any money, now that I think about it," the storyteller said between bites. "They paid in grain that looked like it had been left in the silo too long, plus an old Dollnick colony ship that was parked in orbit around Gnosis Four. I'm not really sure it was theirs, but if there were any sentients left on Four, they didn't complain."

"But in your story, you're the villains," Lynx couldn't restrain herself from saying.

"Yes. Were you only interested in stories where we're the good guys?" The old storyteller appeared to be stumped. "I'm not sure I know any of those."

"Tell them the one about the black hole weapon," the elderly human suggested to a decrepit Frunge, whose vines were withered on his head.

"From the Forgotten Zone?" the Frunge croaked. "That was just a couple years ago. The story hasn't had a chance to ripen."

"It's what they want," the old Drazen woman said. "Besides, you need the practice."

"Our mob had begun tunneling into the Forgotten Zone, just to get away from things for a while, when a young shrub with too much ambition picked up a repeating signal coming from a nearby system. Since the mob expected to spend at least a month in the Zone, getting things in order and choosing our next destination, Pzorat, that was the fool's name, decided to investigate. He was dating a sapling whose father owned an old jump-capable explorer, on which I was unfortunately a guest, and Pzorat basically hijacked the ship with all onboard."

"You weren't able to decode the repeating signal?" Lynx asked.

"Didn't have to," the old Frunge replied. "It was broadcasting in all of the modern languages, including Frunge. Some drivel about the system being a protected galactic historical site and warning visitors not to touch anything. So we ended up in orbit around this cold ball of rock with an unbreathable atmosphere and no intelligent life. Pzorat, who had put a password on the ship controller, refused to return to the mob without visiting the surface."

"What made the world a historical site?" Thomas asked with obvious interest. "Were there abandoned cities, or signs of a devastating war?"

"Signs of a devastating war," the Frunge repeated. "I like that. I'll have to add it to the story."

"You're making this up?" Lynx asked, struggling to contain her frustration.

"Storytellers don't make up stories, just details," the Frunge replied with a certain dignity. "So the kids take the shuttle down to the surface, and for some reason I'll never understand, I agreed to go along for the ride. The next thing I know, I'm in a full environmental suit, staggering along behind these two idiots. The visor keeps fogging up because it was freezing out, and never having worn one before, I didn't know about the defrost. Still, it was something to see, an incredible ceramic city that stretched on forever. There weren't any tall buildings, but the streets were laid out like a grid, and looking down any of them, the view didn't change all the way to the horizon. That's why it didn't look like much from space, because the whole surface was built up the same way."

"I know somebody who would love to visit a world like that," Lynx commented, thinking of Clive. "Do you have the galactic coordinates?"

"There's probably a record on that ship's controller, but they left the mob after that, so your guess is as good as mine," the Frunge croaked complacently. "Now stop interrupting, I'm getting to the good part. These kids had brought some kind of detection device, sort of a hand-held treasure hunter's special that scans for all kinds of elements and compounds. We aren't on the surface a half an hour, and they've collected more ceramic doo-dads than they can carry. I asked what's so special about these, the place is littered with the stuff, you see, and they tell me that they're tools of some kind. Well, I was exhausted by this point and I made sure they knew it, so we go back to the shuttle and return to the explorer ship."

"Didn't you say that the signal warned against touching anything?" Thomas asked.

"It's an old prospector trick, setting up a repeater with a message claiming that some place or another is a galactic historical site under Stryx protection," the old Drazen male answered for the Frunge, who looked quite winded.

"How can you tell a real warning from a fake one?" Thomas asked.

"The Stryx will let you know eventually if you guess wrong," the Drazen replied.

"So, you robbed a historical site and came back with a black hole weapon," Lynx summarized.

"By the time we returned to the explorer with the artifacts, the girl's father had cracked the password on the ship controller, and if his daughter hadn't been on the shuttle with us, we would have been left behind," the old Frunge continued. "Pzorat and the girl lock themselves in the ship's lab and start running all kinds of tests on the artifacts, trying to get them to do something. Crazy kids. I took a nap, and when I woke up, the evacuation alarms were going off and I thought everybody had abandoned ship and left me behind. But it turned out that the kids weren't as dumb as they looked, because when those tools began showing signs of life, they dumped them all in the shuttle and sent it off to a safe distance, watching the artifacts over a comm link."

"How did they know what a safe distance was?" Thomas asked.

"I'm here, aren't I?" the old Frunge snapped. "Anyway, the whole collection of artifacts drew together and began to shrink, never saw anything like it in my life. Then bits and pieces of the shuttle's cabin began flying through the air and sticking to that mass, and they just sort of flattened out. Pretty soon, the hull of the shuttle began to buckle, and before the comm link failed, we saw that everything was vanishing into a sort of a singularity. When the shuttle disappeared from our sensors, we jumped out of there and back to the fleet."

"That's it?" Lynx demanded. "You violated a Stryx warning, stole artifacts from a historical galactic site, and triggered them to do something without a clue about what you were playing with?"

"The character development needs more work," the Frunge admitted. "I should play up the romance angle."

"Were you even really along on the trip?" she asked.

"I knew somebody who was," the Frunge said defensively. "Audiences usually prefer first-person tellings."

"Does anybody have a story about strategic threats or AI running wild that doesn't involve the Wanderers stealing something?" Lynx inquired icily.

"I could tell them my story about how the commune joined the mob," Monos said.

"Not that again," the old Drazen moaned. Several of the other elders ostentatiously put their heads on the table or got up and wandered off.

"It happened at Kalthair Two," the human began. "The crew of the Intrepid had formed a commune to share our compensation, a repurposed colony ship we accepted from the Dollnicks in exchange for labor, and we were using it as a base for asteroid prospecting. Exploring for minerals in a vacuum is hard work, dangerous, and although we had located valuable resources, we lacked the capital to exploit them. Also, the original commune members were feeling their age."

"So are we," the elderly Drazen leader interjected. "Now hurry up with it so we can all go home and take a nap."

"When the Phygorean mob began arriving at Kalthair Two, the commune was just beginning to break up. There were continual arguments over work assignments and the division of recreational resources, and twenty years of slaving together for the Dollnicks wasn't the best preparation for self-government. I was on the first committee to visit the Wanderer fleet, and we were all impressed by what we saw. Unfortunately, there weren't any humans with the mob, so the only way we could join was by bringing our own place to live, and we only had the shared colony ship."

"And you couldn't steal it because it was full of commune members," Lynx guessed.

"There was that," Monos admitted, "but there was also the problem with our work habits. The Wanderers don't have many rules—actually, I take that back, but they aren't the kind of rules you'd expect. The biggest rule is that you can't join the mob if you're going to spend most of your time working just to stay alive, because that just kills the mood for everybody. And the refit of the Intrepid the Dollnicks had done before handing it over was just enough to let us survive in it. Most of our labor went into growing food and doing routine maintenance. It's one of the reasons we weren't getting rich from the mining claim."

"But you did join with the Intrepid," Thomas objected. "We passed it on the way here."

"So we were between a rock and a hard place," the old human continued, ignoring the interruption. "The mob was only going to be around for a few months, and even if we stopped mining and worked on the ship around the clock, we didn't have the tools or the technical skills to bring it up to Wanderer automation standards. We tried listing it on the galactic trade exchange, hoping to swap the Intrepid and the mining claim with humans who had a much smaller colony ship that was in better shape, or even just a decent space habitat without a jump drive."

"Did you ever take a vote about this, or did some of you just decide for the others?" Lynx asked.

"We voted," Monos replied. "It might have been a close thing, but one of our shuttles returning from the mines had recently been destroyed in a freak accident. It ran into fragments from an unexpected collision between a couple of asteroids. It really was a dangerous place to work."

"But how did the Intrepid get upgraded?" Thomas persisted.

"So the only answer that resulted from our advertisement was from a consortium calling itself the Helper AI," the storyteller continued. "They claimed they could upgrade our colony ship to completely automate the farming and maintenance functions, and all they wanted in return was a quitclaim deed for our mines. We took the deal, and the next thing we knew, an enormous hive ship jumped in. I've never seen anything like it before and hope I never will again."

"What's a hive ship?" Lynx asked.

"Looks like it sounds," Monos replied. "Picture a termite mound for insects that work in metal, multiply it by a few billions or trillions, and hope that it doesn't bite. The thing made our Dollnick ship look like a beauty contest winner. It was pure function, just a big ball of robot drones and a place to put them. We were so scared of the thing that we would have backed out of the deal if we could have, but those robots were swarming all over the Intrepid before we had time to act. Big robots, little robots, working around the clock, never saying a word. The whole job took them less than three weeks."

"So the hive took over your mining claim and you were able to join the Wanderers," Thomas concluded.

"That's right," the old man said. "Those drones even fixed up all the empty living space that we'd never gotten around to converting from Dollnick use to human. Can't say anything bad about their work, even the commune members who never wanted the deal had to admit it was a bargain. But for three weeks, those robots must have outnumbered us by hundreds or thousands to one. This was outside of Stryx space, you know, and if the hive queen or whatever AI was running the show had decided to get rid of us and take the ship along with the mine, we would have been dead."

"It's not much of a story," the old Drazen male said with a yawn. "There wasn't a single axe in the whole thing."

The remaining storytellers took the conclusion of the human's story as a signal that the session was at an end, and they began to rise and head home for their naps.

"Thank you," Lynx said to Monos. "That's just the sort of thing we were interested in hearing about. Do you have any others?"

"I think you're a little confused about what storytellers do, young lady," the old human said, struggling to his feet with an assist from Thomas. "Current events are not our thing, too easy to check the facts. You never would have gotten in the door here if the old witch hadn't taken a shine to your pretty-boy pal."

"Bond," Thomas said to Lynx, as they headed back towards the taxi stand. "James Bond."

Nine

"Welcome to the first broadcast of Sentients Match Wits."

Kelly spoke directly to the middle holo-camera, which floated in front of the studio audience. It was hard not to think about the fact that billions of viewers could be watching the live broadcast, and that hundreds of billions more might consume it on demand. Given how the length of the day varied across the species, it was a wonder that anybody watched anything live anymore. Something blurred in the ambassador's vision, and she noticed the frantic Grenouthian director jumping up and down in front of the studio audience.

"We thought it would be fun to launch our show with a guest panel from the diplomatic community," Kelly continued in a rush, trying to make up for the time she had spaced out. "In the future, we'll be choosing panels from the studio audience, so don't forget to ping us at SMW, care of Union Station, for an opportunity to be on the show. Oh, and I'm EarthCent Ambassador Kelly McAllister, if I didn't mention that already."

The Grenouthian director covered his eyes with his hands and sat on the floor, making Kelly wonder if refusing the teleprompts-via-implant option had been a wise choice. The whole opening spiel had been a last-minute idea of the Grenouthian producer, who thought that starting right in with introducing the panels would be too abrupt. Well, they were going to find out.

"Let me introduce the two teams of ambassadors who will be facing off today, starting with the short species." Kelly winced on realizing she had mistakenly used the informal description of the team that she and Aisha had come up with in their practice sessions. "Drazen Ambassador Bork, Frunge Ambassador Czeros, and myself."

Hearing Kelly make the introductions, the technical director swapped to the camera feeds for the "short" panel, where the make-up crew were still applying last-minute touches. Neither of the ambassadors in question realized that they were live. Czeros could be seen taking a slug from a bottle of wine, while a Grenouthian stylist was trying to stuff Bork's tentacle inside the back of his jacket.

"The, uh, other team consists of Dollnick Ambassador Crute, Verlock Ambassador Srythlan, and Grenouthian Ambassador, er, I never did get your name, sir," Kelly concluded lamely. She could just imagine that the first minute of the show would be preserved for all time in entertainment industry training schools as an example of what happens when amateurs try to adlib.

"Just 'Ambassador'," the Grenouthian said coldly. Kelly almost hit herself on the forehead right in front of everybody. How could she forget that the Grenouthians kept their names secret for fear of losing their souls?

"I'll take my place, then," Kelly said, moving to occupy the empty seat between Bork and Czeros. The technical director switched holo-streams several times, from tracking the host's progress, to the tittering studio audience, and back again to the other ambassadors. It seemed to take minutes for Kelly to install herself in place, an action that had been scheduled for the commercial break after her forgotten monologue, but in reality, it only took around thirty seconds. The Grenouthian producer crouched in the corner of the control booth, whimpering.

"Before we begin the first round, I should point out that the questions we'll be asked are taken from the school curriculums of the sentients present. Now, please welcome our special guest moderator, Stryx Jeeves," Kelly concluded, trying to sound as enthusiastic as possible.

There had been quite a bit of discussion with the Grenouthians about how to avoid the great bugaboo of quiz shows around the galaxy, namely, cheating on the questions. The only solution they could agree upon was turning the moderator job over to the Stryx. Once that had been resolved, Kelly would have been happier with Libby picking the questions, but Jeeves had volunteered, and she couldn't think of an excuse to bar the mischievous AI from participating.

"Hello, sentients of the galaxy!" Jeeves blared, arriving center stage between the facing panels with a loud pop. The audience burst into applause for the first time since Kelly had walked onto the stage, and the sudden breeze caused by the Stryx's short hop or supersonic flight from the wings was a welcome relief under the studio lighting. The robot was improbably dressed in a formal tuxedo tailored to his non-humanoid form, complete with a top hat that featured a wrap-around transparent band, since it covered his sensor array and would have otherwise blocked the visual spectrum. After the applause died out, Jeeves continued.

"In addition to asking the questions, I'll be suppressing any attempts by the contestants to consult implant resources or communicate outside of their heads," Jeeves announced, throwing in a spin move just because he could.

"Without further ado, the first question is for Ambassador Crute. On the formerly occupied world of Brupt Minor, the standard mode of communication was telepathy. However, children born without the telepathic facility could be taught to express their thoughts through a loop of string shared and manipulated by two individuals. Demonstrate the method."

"That's not fair," Kelly whispered to Bork. "I don't think the Dollnicks even existed yet when the Stryx drove the Brupt from the galaxy."

"Just watch," Bork replied. He sounded more annoyed with the interruption than concerned about the integrity of the show.

A Grenouthian crew member hopped onto the stage with a large loop of scarlet yarn that he handed to Crute. The Dollnick ambassador casually stretched out the loop between the hands of his upper and lower arms on one side, displayed it to the audience, and then reached over with the hands from the other side, hooking the loop around the wrists. Then he began to move through an intricate set of motions that created, in turn, a cradle, a Brupt Battle sphere, and a Sheezle bug.

"Phenomenal!" Jeeves exclaimed. "A sentient with sentiment. An ambassador who knows his history. A genuine contribution to the diplomatic ranks!"

The studio audience clapped and cheered, the Dollnicks making the most noise of all.

"How did he do that?" Kelly whispered to Bork. Her Drazen friend didn't even look in her direction.

"Our next question is for Ambassador Czeros, and it involves Verlock history. What was the cause of the great revolt of I'npredas, during the reign of Hrrgeraat the Four-hundred and Sixth?"

"Why, every schoolchild knows that," Czeros replied. "The Hrrgeraat rulers on Verlock Prime maintained their grip on power through a monopoly on mercury, a vital nutrient for Verlock children. In the days before the Verlocks developed interplanetary travel, it was thought that all of the mercury sources were located on the Southern continent, but the rebel I'npredas located a new source while investigating the lack of volcanic activity on the hitherto unoccupied Northern land mass. I believe the revolt continued in slow-motion for some ten thousand years, before the Verlocks developed jump drives and the point became moot."

"Correct!" Jeeves shouted, pointing his pincer at Czeros. Kelly stared at the Frunge in amazement. It was hard to picture him knowing the answer to anything that didn't involve wineries or vintages. If these were the kind of questions Jeeves would be asking them all, she was in trouble. The audience applauded again, obviously impressed.

"This next question is for the Grenouthian Ambassador. The Empire of a Hundred Worlds exceeded that number some millions of years ago, but the Vergallians stuck with the name rather than changing it every time they acquired new real estate. What is the current number of worlds in the Vergallian Empire?"

"Please clarify whether you are including twinned-planets and ongoing terraforming projects in the count, or just the current number of unique domains as recognized by Vergallian Heralds," the Grenouthian replied.

"I'll take either answer, providing you tell me which it is," Jeeves said.

"There are currently two hundred and seventy-one Vergallian domains recognized by their College of Heraldry, and another eighty-nine, if we include twinned worlds, dwarf planets and active terraforming missions," the Grenouthian ambassador stated confidently.

"Bingo!" Jeeves hollered, flashing some brilliant emerald lights on his casing that Kelly had never seen in action before. "Correct on both counts."

The studio audience cheered, and the Grenouthian studio crew all whistled loudly, showing their support of the ambassador. The Stryx spun around a few more times, and then approached the "short" panel. The human ambassador felt herself shrinking in her seat, hoping that Jeeves would take pity and not give her one of the impossible questions. The floating robot stopped directly in front of her.

"Bork!" Jeeves said, not even turning in the direction of the Drazen ambassador. "On the Huravian home world, an order of monks is dedicated to the breeding and education of war dogs. Huravian hounds that forge the strongest connections to individuals are known to return after death in the form of puppies reborn on Huravia. Once a reincarnation is identified, the monks escort it to a Stryx station, and provide the dog with just one item. That item is?"

"I know that one!" Kelly said excitedly. "It's…"

"Silence!" Jeeves thundered, pointing a menacing pincer in her direction. The audience all booed, and a few even jeered the human ambassador.

"A begging bowl," Bork answered, as soon as he could be heard. "The emblem on the bowl is a dog looking up at the stars."

"Exactly," Jeeves declared, though he said it rather grimly, with none of the enthusiasm with which he'd greeted the prior correct answers. The audience reacted in accordance with the Stryx's muted response, and other than some polite applause from the few Drazens present, there was silence.

Jeeves floated back over to the other panel and stopped in front of the Verlock, who eyed the Stryx imperturbably.

"Ambassador Srythlan," Jeeves said.

"Yes?" the Verlock replied ponderously.

"On the Farling world of Sixteen, there is a naturally occurring compound..."

"Quadhexseptiumsylleucyglutamyleucine," the Verlock interrupted Jeeves, shocking everyone present with the rapid-fire syllables.

"Winner!" Jeeves practically screamed. "Winner, winner, winner. Oh, the wonders biologicals are showing us today. Now let's ask a question of the new kid on the block, the creator of this show, the inheritor of the Kasilian treasure, and the recent Carnival Queen. The incomparable, Ambassador Kelly McAllister!"

Kelly began to blush halfway through the introduction, though strangely enough, it made her feel cold rather than warm. And when Jeeves finished his build-up, the studio audience remained dead silent. Kelly kicked herself for making her family and friends stay at home. Jeeves approached slowly, allowing the silence to stretch on until it became almost painful.

"Libby!" Kelly subvoced urgently. "What's wrong with Jeeves? Libby? Hello? Gryph?"

It was the first time in fifteen years on the station that Kelly had called out and not received an answer. Suddenly she remembered that Jeeves was jamming their implants to prevent cheating.

"I've changed the rules a little to make your show more interesting," Jeeves said, menace dripping from each syllable. "Answer correctly, and you'll go on to the direct

94

questioning round. Get it wrong, and I promise you a painless transformation into a frog. For all of your marbles, the Oxus Civilization belongs to what historical age on Earth?"

The EarthCent ambassador froze, the threat ringing in her ears. She was sure she knew the answer but she couldn't think, the words just wouldn't come out. She turned desperately to Bork, who was hiding his lips from the Stryx behind a hand and mouthing something at her. Brown? Browse? Brawn? It was on the tip of her tongue. Bra?

Kelly looked down and saw that she was wearing nothing but a bra and panties. Bork leered, and the floating holo-cameras moved in for a close-up as she screamed.

"Five seconds!" Jeeves stated maliciously.

"Kelly," Joe said. "It's all right, I'm here."

"Four! Three!"

"Joe," she sobbed in relief, craning her head to locate him. "What age was the Oxus Civilization?"

"Two! One!"

The crowd screamed for blood, and her face began to turn wet and hot, the beginning of her transformation to amphibian form.

"Kelly! Wake up," her husband shook her shoulder. "You're having another nightmare about the show!"

"Nightmare?" Kelly asked, sitting up in bed. She pushed away Beowulf, who had covered her face and hair with dog slobber in a futile attempt to rouse her by licking.

"I tried to wake you up, but you kept asking me a question about the Oxus Civilization."

"Bronze Age!" Kelly exclaimed. "Why couldn't I remember that a minute ago? Jeeves was going to turn me into a frog."

"And I was going to say you've been spending too much time trying to come up with a plan for your show, but now I'm worried you're spending too much time reading children's books." Joe hugged his wife the best he could while sitting in bed, and began patting her on the back like a child. "The Stryx don't turn people into frogs. That's a fairy tale thing."

"All the other ambassadors knew the answers to the questions Jeeves asked, and most of them were really hard," Kelly recounted. "Then he looked right at me and asked a question about Huravian reincarnation, but it was for Bork."

"What was Jeeves doing on the show in the first place?" Joe asked.

"To keep everybody from cheating," Kelly explained. "When he started acting funny, I tried to contact Libby or Gryph, but he blocked me. And then the whole galaxy saw me in my underwear. It was horrible."

"Listen, Kel. You know I'll support you in anything you do, but I think that maybe your subconscious is trying to tell you something."

"That I'm stupid?" Kelly sat up a little straighter and pushed her husband away. "Is that your interpretation, that I have an inferiority complex? Next time I have a bad dream I'm asking Dring or Libby to do the psychoanalyzing."

"I don't think you have an inferiority complex," Joe protested, trying to get Kelly to turn her head back to look at him. "I think it's a performance anxiety dream. You're great at standing up and speaking your mind when you have to, and I've even seen you give a couple of decent speeches, but you've never been an actor, a performer. It's not that I think you're trying to compete with Aisha, but it does seem that in all of the show ideas you come up with, you cast yourself in the role of a participant, or even the master of ceremonies."

"I was both in this one," Kelly admitted. "I completely flubbed my opening, but I don't remember the details now."

"You don't see the Grenouthian ambassador appearing on the shows he helps develop," Joe said. "If things are really so slow around the embassy that you need another job, talk to Clive and tell him to start sending more of the aliens who contact EarthCent Intelligence your way."

"Maybe you're right," Kelly replied, and let out a long sigh. "I do keep trying to give myself a part, and perhaps I am a little jealous of Aisha. I'm going to start auditioning human moderators so I don't have to participate on camera."

That'll be a welcome relief, Beowulf thought, as he padded back to Dorothy's room where he had claimed most of the floor space. A growing dog can only take so many of these middle-of-the-night interruptions.

Ten

"Thank you again for not inviting your Mom," Mist told Dorothy. "It wouldn't have been much fun for everybody if we had two ambassadors, and Gwendolyn would have been disappointed if I didn't ask her."

"It's not a Parents Day, it's a Career Day. It's just for us grown-up kids," Dorothy explained. "And when I was little and Mom came to Parents Day, it didn't go that well."

"And when I was young, I never got to invite anybody for Parents Day," Metoo added, hoping that his own history would reassure Mist in case she felt left out. "You can invite anybody you want for Career Day, even sentients from different species. But I found out there's never been Stryx for Career Day before, so I asked Jeeves."

"It might have been better to ask somebody else," Dorothy said. "It's not as if biologicals who study really hard can grow up to get work as Stryx."

"Shhh. Gwendolyn's here," Mist said to her friends. The class, ranging from ages twelve to fourteen, were lounging around on the grass in the presentations area, propping themselves partially upright with pillows and beanbags. The number of Stryx who participated in classes began to fall off around the age of ten, but those who could visit Union Station on short notice still came for the school's special events to keep up with their human friends. There weren't any parents present.

98

"Hello, students," Gwendolyn said, as she moved uncertainly to the front of the group. "I don't see a teacher here. Should I just begin?"

"You're the first today," answered a boy who was sitting cross-legged near the front. "You get to make your own rules on Career Day, but you can't go over ten minutes with the questions and answers. Your sponsor should introduce you."

"I was about to, Maximilian, before you interrupted," Mist said, clambering to her feet. The class was just getting to the age where the boys and girls took great satisfaction in telling one another how they should act. "I invited my sister Gwendolyn to talk about her work. She's the Gem Ambassador on Union Station."

The children applauded politely.

"Well, this sounds fun," the clone said. "Should I talk about being an ambassador?"

"We had one of those already," a girl called out. "It was yucky. Have you done anything else?"

"We're grown-ups now, Bekka," Dorothy told the girl. "This ambassador isn't going to make us play games."

"I don't have to talk about being an ambassador," Gwendolyn said. "I've only been one for a couple of years and I usually don't know what I'm doing. I used to be a waitress. Do you want to hear about that?"

"Yes!" Bekka answered. "My sister is a waitress and she makes oodles of creds in tips."

Gwendolyn exchanged a significant look with Mist, communicating through a mix of body language, empathy, and a bit of clone telepathy, to make sure the subject was alright with her. Mist shrugged, a sign even Dorothy could understand.

"To give you a little background, when I was just about your age, I started working on the Gem crèche world with babies," Gwendolyn began. "But the supervisors said that I was too sentimental to work with the little ones, so they sent me for waitress training."

"Do you need training to be a waitress?" a different girl asked. "I thought you just had to memorize the specials and stuff."

"You need training for all jobs," the Gem replied. "Sometimes it's formal training, like in a school, and sometimes it's on-the-job."

"But you get paid for on-the-job training, right?" Bekka asked.

"On Union Station you do," Gwendolyn replied. "That's because the Stryx have labor laws for the multi-species decks, so if your own species wasn't willing to pay, you could usually find a better job just a lift tube ride away."

"But the Gem Empire didn't pay anybody for anything," Mist added.

"Well, not in the way business works on the station," Gwendolyn said, clarifying Mist's words. "In the old Gem Empire, everybody got a job and everybody had to work. If you didn't show up for work, you couldn't go to the dining halls or the clothing warehouses. The Gem who were in charge, the elites, got better rooms, and access to better dining halls and better warehouses, but nobody got paid in creds. We didn't even have our own form of money."

"Weird!" said the boy sitting up front. "We know that barter is better, but how can you save for retirement or travel without money?"

"There wasn't any retirement, really," Gwendolyn explained. "And there wasn't any stuff to buy either, just the places you were allowed to go and get stuff, depending on your job."

"And you didn't get an allowance?" a girl asked incredulously. "How could you go out with your friends, or rent flying wings? Were your parents that mean?"

"Lydia!" Dorothy scolded the girl. "Weren't you listening when Libby introduced Mist to the class? They're clones."

"So?" Lydia responded in a huff. "If I was a clone, I'd still give my daughter an allowance."

"You're both right, so please don't argue," Gwendolyn interjected. "Dorothy is correct that we don't have parents because we're all sisters, and Lydia is correct that the older sisters act as parents for the younger. But when you're just a child in crèche, you don't understand that the food from the dining hall and the clothes from the warehouse are actually gifts from your older sisters. It's just the way things work, so it seems as if the Empire is your mother. Humans have parents or guardians who take care of you when you're too young to take care of yourself, so you form family bonds with them. Gem children were taught that everything came from the Empire, and we were prohibited from making friends with anybody outside of our caste."

"So you never made any tips as a waitress?" Bekka asked, getting to the crux of the matter.

"No," Gwendolyn replied. "When I started, we didn't even get to eat the same food as the upper castes we served, because our meals were from a different self-service dining hall."

"No wonder the waitresses led the revolution," Bekka exclaimed. "If my sister had to wait on people who got better food than her and never tipped, she would have put sleeping drugs in their food too!"

"You might not believe me, but the job was better before the whole Empire shifted to the all-in-one nutrition drink," Gwendolyn told them. "After that, all we did was count people and bring out glasses on a tray. At least back when they were ordering fancy food, I could smell it, and imagine that one day somebody might leave an uneaten portion on the plate. Without different types of food to remember and describe to patrons, waitressing was incredibly boring. The best thing is if you can find work that's challenging."

"That's what Libby says," Maximilian observed. "I think it's around ten minutes," he added.

"I was about to tell her that," Mist exclaimed in annoyance.

"Thank you for having me," Gwendolyn concluded, wondering why Kelly had warned her against ever participating in a Stryx school event. The children applauded enthusiastically, and Mist sat up very straight, sharing in her sister's success.

"I'm next," Metoo called out, rising up and floating above the other students. "I mean, Jeeves is next. He's my Career Day display."

"Thank you, Metoo," Jeeves bellowed, zooming up to the front at break-neck speed the moment the introduction was completed. Metoo settled back into his place next to Dorothy. "As the first Stryx to attend Libby's experimental school, I'm honored to be invited back for this special event."

"But you don't have to work," a boy in the back objected. "You're Stryx."

"You don't have to work either," Jeeves retorted. "You can run away from home and join the Wanderers. Oops, Libby just told me to say I didn't mean that. Besides, I started working when I was younger than you. All Stryx do."

"But we can't hope to be chosen to rule a whole species as High Priest, like Metoo," a girl pointed out.

"Do you think that's the only career path open to Stryx?" Jeeves parried. "I'll even let you choose which one of my careers to talk about. I've been the chief trouble-shooter for the Eemas dating service, an auctioneer, and I'm a member of Galaxy Watch."

"You worked for Eemas?" Bekka asked. "I want to hear about that."

"What's Galaxy Watch?" Maximilian demanded.

"Galaxy Watch consists of a heavily armed and danger-ous group of intrepid warrior AI who defend the tunnel network from—what do you mean the subject is out of bounds?" Jeeves trailed off in complaint. "Libby told me to stop exposing her censorship and to talk about the dating service."

"Wow, Jeeves is really cool," said the boy sitting behind Metoo, nudging the robot.

"Can you find me a boy who doesn't smell funny?" a girl called out, leading the other girls in the class to col-lapse into giggles.

"If I still worked for Eemas, I could find you a boy who smelled any way you like," Jeeves replied. "It's one of the gazillions of factors we considered when making introduc-tions."

"Gazillions?" Dorothy asked skeptically. "The way my mom described her dates, it sounded more like Eemas was picking guys at random. They weren't even all human."

"The ambassador was part of the special remedial dating program," Jeeves explained. "All of the other species on the station sign up with a dating service to find their best match, but some humans can't coherently describe what they want for breakfast, much less for the rest of their lives. So rather than wasting the ideal match for humans on the first date and risking a rejection, we try to use the early dates as a training program."

"That sounds like the sort of thing Libby would do," Bekka commented.

"Does a dating service troubleshooter ever get to shoot anybody?" Maximilian asked.

Rather than replying with words, Jeeves projected a hologram of himself mounted on the hull of the Nova, firing an energy beam weapon at a Sharf cabin cruiser and scoring a direct hit on the propulsion system. The boys in the class all whooped and shouted. That hologram was immediately replaced by another, this one showing a full-fledged space battle between small robots and some type of massive ship none of the kids recognized. The caption "Galaxy Watch" flashed at the bottom, but the projection was quickly extinguished.

"Oops, how did that get onto my dating service reel?" Jeeves said innocently, after the boys calmed down. "I'd show you more, but you know who is you know what."

"Did any of the dates Eemas sent people on result in marriages instead of battles?" a fourteen-year-old girl in the back asked icily.

"Practically all of them," Jeeves replied. "The Eemas service had a success rate near a hundred percent before humans came to the station, but you people are tough. I got the job as troubleshooter because after attending this school, I was better at predicting human behavior at the individual level than the other Stryx. When things weren't working out and I was called in, I'd start knocking heads together," he concluded on a macho note.

"What about love?" the girl followed up.

"You're not my type," Jeeves responded, drawing a big laugh from the boys. "Seriously, though. You humans make a big deal out of love, like it's some sort of magical gift of the gods rather than something you choose to do for reasons you prefer not to acknowledge. I'll bet you a hundred creds I can predict who you're going to mar— what? Never mind."

"I'm sorry, students," Libby said, addressing the class directly for the first time that day. "I'm afraid that Jeeves isn't as mature as you'd expect for a twenty-six-year-old Stryx who has instant access to tens of millions of years of memories and who also doesn't sleep."

"She's implying I've lived thirty-eight years by staying up nights," Jeeves explained, in case the kids didn't get it. A new hologram appeared, this one of a giant hook, and it stayed right with Jeeves as he tried to bob and weave away from it.

"Thank you for coming, Jeeves," Metoo said, floating up from the grass. "Libby says it's been ten minutes."

"Has not," Jeeves muttered, giving in and moving off in the hook's embrace. He drew a rousing round of applause from the boys, and nasty looks from those girls who didn't choose to ignore him.

"Chastity?" Dorothy called out, looking around. "Are you here yet?"

Chastity approached from the back along with Marcus, whom she had finally tempted into visiting Union Station with the promise of seeing the Stryx experimental school she attended as a girl. Dorothy had originally invited

Blythe for career day, but when Chastity heard about it, she asked to switch.

"Hi, kids," Chastity said, making her way through the children to the front. "Wow, Career Day. It feels like just last year I was sitting where you are."

"You're much older than that," Bekka informed her.

"This is Chastity, and you all know about her because she runs InstaSitter," Dorothy said, popping up to give the introduction and then immediately sitting back down.

"I thought you were inviting the spy sister," Maximilian complained, drawing a chorus of support from the boys.

"She's taking care of her twins," Chastity replied for Dorothy. "Do you want me to tell her to come and bring the Terrible Twos? Maybe you could take care of them while she talks?"

"I'm fine with you," the boy said hastily.

"Alright, so that was the introduction, and I'm going to talk about business for those of you who are ambitious," Chastity said.

"Who's he?" a girl asked, pointing at Marcus.

"Probably her Eemas date," Maximilian said in a stage whisper.

"Marcus is my friend from the mob, and I brought him to see how..."

"He's a Wanderer?" Bekka interrupted.

"Yes, I just said that," Chastity replied impatiently. "Now we only have ten minutes so..."

"I heard the Wanderers don't have careers," a boy interrupted from the back.

"That's crazy," a girl next to him retorted. "Everybody has to work."

"I don't work," Marcus said, and launched into the same explanation he had given Blythe and Clive about the

106

importance of leisure. Chastity stepped back, looking amused as he attempted to show how the Wanderers maintain the balance in galactic energy by offsetting the grim workaholic natures of the busy-beaver species.

"Do you really believe that crap?" Maximilian asked.

"Don't say 'crap,'" Bekka reprimanded him, throwing her lawn pillow at his back.

"Of course I believe it," Marcus declared, looking more shocked than offended. "I know you all have homes here so you have to act like they tell you, but wouldn't you really rather be playing all day?"

"Like babies?" Dorothy suggested. Mist and several of the other kids who caught the implication snickered, but Marcus was so used to sharing his views with like-minded Wanderers that the insult went right over his head.

"Who wouldn't want to be a baby again?" he replied with a dreamy smile. "You get fed, clothed, you can sleep any time you want, and all you have to do if you want attention is cry."

"So we can change your diaper?" Bekka asked, at which point the whole class broke out laughing, including Chastity.

"Oh, I think little Marcus is going to cry," a boy called out.

"No, he's just cranky because he missed his nap," Mist ventured.

"I started working with Metoo when I was five," Dorothy stated proudly. "You're like, old already, and you've never worked?"

"I dance," Marcus said, but he was starting to look around like he was seeking an exit from a trap. "Without dancing, what joy would there be in life? And I cook pretty well, but only for friends."

"Have you ever earned even a single cred?" Bekka demanded.

"I, this isn't, Chastity, you explain it to them," Marcus stuttered.

"I'd have to understand it to explain it," Chastity replied. She should have known better than to doubt Libby's dating advice. If anything was going to bring Marcus around to reality, shock treatment at the hands of school kids was the best bet.

"I'm a good guy," Marcus defended himself desperately. "I always put my dirty utensils in the right bins so the dishwasher bot doesn't have to sort them. I don't sit around all day plugged into virtual reality like some people, I get out and mingle. I've been cleaning my own room since I was, uh, twenty. Once, when the woman on our corridor who has a child asked me for help, I even babysat for a couple hours."

"Wow, you're practically an InstaSitter," Maximilian said sarcastically.

"Why did you make it sound like there's only one woman on your corridor with a kid?" Mist asked. "Is the corridor that short?"

"No, there are twenty units on my stub," Marcus answered, seizing on the question that could be easily answered. "Wanderers don't have many children, you know. That's why we always have room for new people to join."

"We didn't know," Bekka said in her most sophisticated tone. "Please enlighten us."

"Well, children are a lot of work," Marcus began to explain. He didn't get any further before he was buried in a volley of pillows.

Eleven

"I'm sorry if I seem a bit out of it," Kelly apologized to the hologram of EarthCent's president, after the other members of the intelligence steering committee signed off of the holo-conference call. "I've been going nuts with preparations for the show, and I just lost track of time."

"The meeting went fine," President Beyer told her. "It's good to know that the Wanderers won't be coming to Earth during my lifetime. I asked you to stay live to discuss three things the others don't need to know about right now. Just hold on a minute so I can find my notes, I have them written down."

"Take your time, Mr. President," Kelly replied. "And if I may say so without sounding rude, am I ever relieved that the Stryx promoted you after President Lin gave up trying to resign and ran away. If it was me in your shoes, I would have hired bounty hunters to track him down."

"You might be surprised to hear this, but I never really got used to living on a station," the new EarthCent president responded. "I would have volunteered to come back to Earth and take this job if it wasn't for the title."

"I can imagine," Kelly said sympathetically. "It's bad enough when I have to introduce myself to new aliens as the EarthCent ambassador, and they ask if we're the Stryx tourist agency for Earth."

"The polite ones ask that." The president sighed as he examined and discarded another scrap of paper. "The others have their preconceived notions about Stryx pets and leave it at that. Ah, here we are," he declared, holding up a ketchup stained napkin with a few words scrawled on it in pen. "Helpers, trainee and questions."

"Was I supposed to understand that and answer?" Kelly asked.

"That's my personal shorthand," Stephen responded. "I wanted to discuss the Helper AI, getting you a new trainee, and your development efforts on this new show for the Grenouthians."

"I think I went over everything I've heard about the Helper AI in the meeting just now," Kelly said. "EarthCent Intelligence has flagged the subject for further investigation, in part because their current information is based on what some old storyteller told our agents."

"It could turn out to be nothing, but I had a visit from one of the Helper AI representatives this week. A rather unnerving experience," the president said. "I can't be sure we're talking about the same group, and of course, this was before I received the intelligence assessment, but the pitch sounded pretty similar."

"The Stryx cleared them through the tunnel?" Kelly asked in surprise. "I thought they had Earth under foreign AI ban so only our own artificial people are allowed through."

"I don't believe the Stryx did let them through, and perhaps I shouldn't say I had a visit when it was more likely a hologram that was just too real for me to detect," the President replied. "I checked with our security after the encounter, and they hadn't recorded anybody entering or leaving my office. So it was either a projection or some sort of material transfer, either of which is beyond our technical capability to detect."

"What did the Stryx say?" Kelly inquired, realizing right after she said it that it was the second time in a row that she had invoked the Stryx.

"Earth isn't a station where you have a first generation Stryx and probably a few offspring around all the time," the president reminded her. "The AI running the space elevators are just short-timers paying off body mortgages. I send a lot of questions to my former Stryx librarian on Void Station, sometimes I even make a tunneling call if I'm desperate, and he hasn't let me down yet. But I get the feeling that the Stryx would prefer if I just muddle through with Earth's resources or work through the ambassadors."

"Then I'm doubly glad you got stuck with the job because I couldn't imagine going a day without talking to our librarian," Kelly said. "In fact, I'll discuss the whole situation with Libby later today and get back to you, since she's no doubt listening in already. I'll try to get Blythe and Clive here for it as well."

"You haven't even heard the AI's proposal yet," Stephen reminded her.

"Oh, right," Kelly replied guiltily. "Whether your visitor was real or just a hologram, what did the manifestation have to say for itself?"

"Quite an offer, really," the president replied. "In exchange for material resources in the solar system, he promised to provide nearly unlimited free labor and technological support that would put us on par with some of the more backwards advanced species. A bit too good to be true, if you ask me."

"Did you get any clarification on what resources they were requesting?" Kelly asked.

"That's where it got a bit sticky," the president confessed. "While my visitor proved difficult to pin down, I believe he was asking for exclusive rights to the asteroid belt and either an inner planet or one of the larger of Jupiter's moons. I got the impression that he was really keen on Mercury, so perhaps they need a lot of heat or solar energy for their operations."

"They want a planet! What did you say?"

"I told him that it was a very interesting offer and if he would provide his contact information, I'd get back to him after conferring with my colleagues.

"And what did he say?" Kelly demanded.

"He said that he was going to be out of the office for an extended period on a business trip, but he'd be happy to swing by on his way back through our space in a few months."

"I thought that the Wanderers would be unwelcome guests, but I'd take them any day over some AI that moves in, wants part of the solar system, and never leaves."

"My feelings exactly, but I'll reserve judgment until all the facts are in," the president concluded. "Now the next item was getting you a new trainee."

"I know I've been stretching a little to get the new show together, but once it's running smoothly, it should only take a few hours a week of my time," Kelly said. "The whole idea is to extend EarthCent's brand of diplomacy in the public awareness. Some of the aliens may look down on us as Stryx pets, but if I've learned one thing in the last few years, it's that everybody wants to be on holo-casts."

"I'm not worried about how you do your job," the president chided her. "I'm perfectly aware that between your office manager and EarthCent Intelligence, you could sneak away from the embassy for a long vacation and nobody would be the wiser. Now, from what I can discover, your last intern was never really intended for the diplomatic service. The Stryx seem to have handpicked her for other reasons and rigged the assignment. The issue is that you are a valuable resource to us, and that resource is going to waste if you aren't passing your skills on to the next generation of diplomats."

"Oh, that's kind of flattering, I guess," Kelly replied. She really didn't know what she would do with another diplomat in the embassy, but she wasn't going to argue with the president's assessment of her value as a mentor. "Will you be sending me somebody from the next training class?"

"I thought it would make more sense to give you a seasoned assistant, one who shows every indication of becoming a career diplomat," Stephen said. "His name is Daniel Cohan, and he was posted to Middle Station the last two years as an acting junior consul. We promoted him to full junior consul on accepting this assignment."

"Well, I'm looking forward to meeting him, though I don't know what he's going to do for work," Kelly said. "Maybe we can send him on diplomatic missions to some of the aliens in this sector who aren't on the tunnel network. When can I expect him?"

"I'm not sure about the exact date," the president said. "He had several months of accumulated vacation time and unpaid educational leave saved up, and he said something about living the life of the mind until his money ran out. I think you'll like him."

"Alright, that's two things. What was the third?"

"As you know, I am in full agreement with the ambassadors on our Intelligence committee that any publicity for EarthCent diplomatic efforts is good publicity. Humans lack the commercial presence to gain visibility on any of the alien worlds where we don't have expatriates working as cheap labor. The first thing I did when I accepted this job was to add an outreach office, for which I hired a former marketing executive from Bill's Exchange. She doesn't need the money, of course. She's doing it for the challenge."

"Doing what, exactly?" Kelly asked.

"Well, her first task was to measure the level of human species recognition among the aliens on the tunnel network. She put some of her own money into hiring subcontractors on a sampling of representative worlds and outposts to do surveys, since the only way to measure success in a promotional campaign is to establish a baseline."

"Well, I guess that sounds smart, though I'm not sure what it is we're supposed to be promoting," Kelly said. "Are there any results yet?"

"Oh yes. The data started coming in almost as soon as she made the payments," President Beyer replied. "It turns out that most species have marketing firms measuring this sort of thing on a continual basis, and if Hildy can convince them that humans have enough disposable income to be of interest, we'll be able to establish reciprocal arrangements in the future."

"Hildy?"

"Hildy Greuen, our new outreach executive," Stephen said. "The data confirmed what several of us had already guessed. The best known human business is InstaSitter, even though they've limited their operations to the stations. The most widely recognized human face is your daughter-in-law's, thanks to her show, and the most significant event people associate with the human race is still the Kasilian auction that you conducted on Union Station."

"With any luck, we'll have a hit with Sentients Match Wits, and the numbers will start moving up," Kelly said. She tried to channel the can-do attitude of the Grenouthian producer responsible for her project.

"Yes, there's that." The president sounded a little hesitant, and then he spoke in a rush. "Hildy thinks it would be highly beneficial if you could make the EarthCent brand as prominent as possible on the show. She says that the subtle approach doesn't work with marketing."

"What did she have in mind, specifically?" Kelly asked. She didn't want to sound thin-skinned, but she worried about somebody she had never met making new demands on her as-of-yet unproven creative ability.

"One idea was to go with a title like, 'EarthCent Quiz Show.' Another was to have a segment where the questions every week pertain to humans. She thought we might supply Earth products as gift items for the correct answers, like Vermont maple syrup or genuine Swiss watches. Maybe the questions could be tied to a different export item for each show."

"She's not shy about trying to do her job, I'll give her that," Kelly said. "We were already planning to include a sort of human trivia question in the show each week, and the gift idea for participants isn't bad. I asked a few of my alien colleagues about what shows they and their families watch, and most of it is pretty corny. There's even a Dollnick show where the contestants basically chase around a maze collecting giant bugs, and the only prize is they get to eat what they catch."

"People need to relax," the president observed. "I suspect it's the same with most sentients, except perhaps the

Wanderers, who seem to be in a permanent state of relaxation."

"I'll try to get the product placements past the Grenouthians," Kelly said. "Remember, they're the ones financing the production. I'll ask about putting EarthCent in the show title, but I don't know. I'm sure the only reason they've tolerated my lack of professionalism to this point is because Aisha's show is such a huge hit. Since they don't really understand why, they're inclined to give me extra elbow room."

"Great, I'll let you go then," the president said enthusiastically. "Don't be surprised if Hildy wants to deliver your goodies in person. She claims she misses traveling for business."

"We always have space, as long as she doesn't mind dogs and kids. Oh, and did I mention that Aisha has unofficially adopted a little Vergallian girl who was abandoned on her set?"

"No, you didn't," Stephen responded. "Perhaps if your show is a success, you'll have the opportunity to adopt a grown-up alien."

"Uh, thanks," Kelly said, signing off without asking where that suggestion came from. Stephen Beyer had been one of the founding ambassadors of the EarthCent Intelligence committee that launched humanity into the espionage game, but he had always struck her as a bit odd. Still, she assumed the Stryx knew what they were doing when they tapped him for president, and most importantly, they hadn't manipulated her into taking the job.

"Clive is waiting in the outer office," Libby announced. "I took the liberty of contacting him when you mentioned that you intended to meet with us after the call. Blythe didn't want to ask anybody to babysit the twins on short notice."

"Clive can fill her in later," Kelly replied, rising and heading for the door. She hesitated for a moment. "Is that selfish of me? Should I tell her to just bring the Things?"

"If you mean my goddaughter and godson, Blythe mentioned that they were all getting ready for a nap in any case," Libby replied haughtily.

With a hand gesture, the ambassador deactivated the security lock that she only used during sensitive holo-conferences, and the door slid open. Clive and Donna were chatting together, and either he or Libby had also pinged Lynx and Thomas, since both were waiting as well.

"Great, everybody I wanted to see," Kelly said. Then she flushed when she realized her words could be interpreted to mean she was relieved the twins were absent. "I mean, I didn't think of asking Lynx and Thomas, but of course, you two were the ones who heard the Helper AI story first hand."

"It's okay," Clive said. "Blythe and I talked it over, and she's going to stop bringing the twins to meetings. Some people just find them too distracting. Besides, in a few more weeks the InstaSitter ban will expire and we're going to start paying for two sitters at a time."

"Why not three, so one can always be on break?" Lynx suggested.

"We may as well meet out here rather than moving all the chairs into my office," Kelly said, ignoring Lynx's attempt to milk the twins topic. "Libby will be participating as well. I just got off a very interesting holo-conference with the home office. It turns out that your Helper AI, or something that acted very similar, recently showed up on Earth. They offered everything from a tech upgrade to unlimited labor, in return for the asteroid belt between Mars and Jupiter, plus one of the smaller planets."

"But I thought artificial people were the only AI allowed to visit Earth," Thomas protested.

"It isn't clear whether the president's visitor was physically present or a long-distance projection," Libby said. "But the offer itself represents the intent to violate our protectorate, which means we'll be investigating."

"Investigating?" Lynx asked skeptically. "As in, you don't know the answer already?"

"Stryx are hardly omniscient," Libby replied calmly. "To the best of our limited knowledge, omniscience on a universal scale isn't possible, as developing the capacity to be omniscient would just lead to more physical states that would have to be known."

"So you've never heard of the Helper AI?" Clive asked.

"They've popped up a couple times over the last few hundred years or so, mainly doing transport barters, but nothing quite as extraordinary as the offer to the EarthCent president," Libby replied. "New forms of AI are always coming and going. Some of them follow stable strategies for growth, others find existence unbearable and self-terminate, a few turn into problems. We try to give them the same opportunity as biologicals to get their act together in privacy before debuting on the galactic stage."

"Will we be stepping on your toes if we investigate independently?" Clive asked.

"Not at this stage," Libby replied. "We would certainly tell you if it was an issue. In fact, I discussed it with Gryph as soon as I heard about the offer to EarthCent, and he delegated the task to Jeeves, so perhaps you can cooperate. After his performance at my school the other day, I suspect he could do with a little action."

Twelve

"It looks to me like a simple pile swap," Joe said. He closed the hologram of the Drazen vessel he'd been studying as they approached the cluster of mammoth colony ships which had been joined together to create one huge habitat. "The Drazen manufacturer promised if the job gets approved, they'll pay us handling fees for receiving the shipment at Mac's Bones, in addition to our regular service rate. Since Gryph clamped down on the ferrying business to prevent all the counterfeit creds from trickling into the station, we've got the extra time. As long as we have the Nova and the space in Mac's Bones, I'm not ready to hang up my tools."

"I still don't get why Bork would call you to quote a repair for the Drazen Wanderers, or why he said you'd be doing him a personal favor." Paul was inclined to be cautious about anything concerning the Wanderers, though brokering an expensive pile on credit provided by the Drazen embassy sounded like a sure thing.

"I asked him about that," Joe said, as Paul matched the spin rate of the habitat and eased the tug towards the universal docking arm. "According to Bork, the Wanderers have been known to entice visiting workers away from their families, and he doesn't want to have to explain himself to any angry spouses. He also said that Wanderer ships tend to be pretty jury-rigged, and the Drazen mechanics on the station are all by-the-book guys."

"Well, nobody can ever accuse you of working by-the-book," Paul replied with a grin. The docking arm airlock locked onto the port of the Nova, and the ship gave a small but noticeable lurch as the two masses became a rigid system. "But why did you think that bringing Beowulf along would be a good idea?"

"That was actually your wife's suggestion, though he needs the Zero-G practice if he's ever going to get his space legs," Joe told his foster son. "I guess Aisha was worried you'd run into a cute Wanderer girl, so she sent the dog along to drag you home."

"Either that or she wants to get rid of both of us, now that she has Ailia." Paul delivered the line lightly, but Joe saw right through his attempted bravado.

"It's just that the poor kid needs so much right now, and your wife thinks she's the only one who can supply it," Joe explained. "I've even seen Aisha looking jealous when I talk with the girl in Vergallian. She does the same thing with Woojin. It's too bad you forgot how to speak it because you were pretty good for a while back when you were around ten."

"Never had a need for it until now," Paul said, loosening his safety harness and rising from the pilot's chair. "I would never say anything against keeping her. The girl is as timid as a mouse, and she tries so hard to please that it breaks my heart at times. I just worry what will happen when she comes of age if she doesn't have an upper caste Vergallian woman to teach her to control those pheromones."

"That's a good twenty years off so I wouldn't worry about it," Joe told Paul. "Have you forgotten that they mature about half as fast as humans and live four times as long?"

"I hadn't thought of that," Paul replied, sounding relieved. "Make sure that Kelly knows. I think she's a bit worried about the girl's effect on Samuel if Aisha and I keep her and we don't move out of your quarters."

Joe released Beowulf from the training net that kept the dog from flying around the cabin during the Zero-G flip between Union Station and the Wanderer mob. The dog remembered all the weightless time he'd spent coasting in space with the mercenaries in his previous life, and he also remembered hating every minute of it. Why the humans didn't maintain a constant rate of acceleration to provide a uniform weight all of the time was beyond him, but he guessed it had to do with money. From a dog's perspective, humans were cheapskates. If Beowulf had been running the show, it would have been steak for breakfast, lunch and dinner.

"I hope there's somebody here to meet us," Paul said over his shoulder to Joe. He stepped into the airlock and tried to squint through the pitted glass window into the Drazen habitat. "You'd think that people in need of an emergency pile swap would at least send a tech to show us where it is."

"I'm sure if we just wander around for a few minutes, somebody will point the way," Joe reassured him. "You and I might not draw much notice, but how many Huravian hounds can there be on board?"

The three exited the airlock and almost tripped over a furry octopus that was waiting to greet them. The short creature wore a sort of harness, to which a wide array of tools were attached by small reels, similar to the type Joe used himself when working in Zero-G. The octopus tilted towards them, leading both humans to bow politely in return. Then it tipped back and forward again, at which point they realized it was working to maintain its balance on a small unicycle. Beowulf whined and hid his head behind Paul.

"Greetings," Joe ventured. "Can I assume you're here to meet us about the estimate for a new pile?"

"Ah, human," the creature replied in scratchy English through a translation device. "Please forgive my mechanical speaking contrivance, we Zarents do not vocalize in a way your implants would recognize. I am an engineer for the habitat chain of which this colony ship is a part. Please follow me and I will take you to the pile."

Without waiting for an answer, the Zarent turned about and pedaled off, impatient to be moving in a straight line again rather than trying to balance in place. The two humans and the giant dog set off after him, discovering they needed to walk at a rapid clip to keep up. They found themselves moving through a park-like environment, the inside surface of the outer hull of the spinning colony ship. Campsites abounded, with groups of Drazens lounging about outside of their traditional round tents, eating and drinking. A few of them pointed at the Huravian hound and made comments to each other, but the humans and the furry octopus on the unicycle passed unnoticed.

"Looks like we're headed for the lift tubes," Paul commented.

"If that little fellow can use all of those tentacles at the same time, he must be a crackerjack Zero-G mechanic," Joe said, huffing a bit to keep up with the Zarent.

Suddenly, Beowulf lunged passed them, going airborne to snatch a piece of meat tossed in their direction by a Drazen campfire chef. All of the Wanderers who were watching the giant dog hooted their appreciation as he made the snag and swallowed.

"Chew your food, boy," Joe said to the dog. "You'll enjoy it more."

Beowulf leapt into the air again, snatching another piece of meat and swallowing it whole once more. He gave Joe a triumphant grin.

"I guess his method has its pluses as well," Paul said. "Keep the decks clear so you'll always have room for cargo."

The trio followed the Zarent past the bank of lift tubes, and continued through a rougher area of terrain, where teams of mechanicals were working at removing old stubble and tilling the soil for a planting. Above their heads, a different crew of mechanicals was replacing burnt-out lights in the ceiling. Another little octopus on a floater appeared to be supervising the job.

"Service entrance," the Zarent announced, wheeling into a large lift tube that stood alone and looked like it had seen better days. "Direct access to the inter-deck utility levels and engineering."

"I've never heard of Zarents before," Paul said, in an attempt to get a conversation going with the little creature. Inside the lift, the Zarent climbed down from the unicycle seat, and with its furry tentacles folded underneath, it barely came up to Paul's knees. In fact, up close and stationary, it looked a bit more like a giant tarantula than an octopus, though neither semblance was more than a human attempt to make the alien seem familiar.

"Not heard of the Zarents?" the creature creaked. "You must not have spent much time around Wanderers."

"We haven't," Joe said. "I was out with my wife for the envoy's reception, but other than that, neither of us has spent any time with the mob. We did keep pretty busy shuttling folks back and forth before the Stryx clamped down."

"Problems with counterfeiting?" the Zarent asked, showing curiosity for the first time.

"You got that right," Joe answered, crouching down and sticking out a hand. "I'm Joe McAllister, this is my son Paul, and that's Beowulf."

The Zarent studied Joe's hand for a moment, and then tentatively swiped it with an appendage. Paul crouched down and went through a similar procedure. Beowulf remained at the far side of the lift capsule, looking doubtful.

"I am third engineer Koffern," the Zarent said, after puzzling out the meaning of the ritual.

"Pleased to meet you, Koffern," Joe responded, straightening up.

"Ah, you misunderstand," the Zarent said to Joe. "This colony ship is the Koffern, I am her third engineer. It is how we designate ourselves."

"Gottcha," Joe replied easily. "Do you have a nickname you go by, something shorter than your full title?"

The little multi-limbed mechanic seemed to hesitate for a moment. Then he replied modestly, "My friends call me 'Giant' because I am the smallest of my age group. It is a sort of humor," the Zarent added by way of explanation, in case the humans were dimwits.

"Giant. That's what we'll call you then," Joe said. "Do you call this service lift Speedy?"

The Zarent rose up on all of its tentacle-like legs and made a clicking sound beneath its body. Beowulf tensed, and the fur on the back of his neck stood up, but Giant soon lowered himself back to the floor.

"That is an excellent joke," the Zarent declared. Apparently its clicking display was the creature's version of laughter. "I will have to tell my friends. The service lift is indeed slow, and it would be even slower if I operated it within the safety specs for its age. You will find that all of the equipment on the Koffern is in a similar state, as are the other colony ships in our habitat cluster, and most of the vessels in the mob."

"Don't you maintain them?" Paul asked, then immediately regretted the seeming rudeness of his question. The Zarent, however, didn't indicate the slightest offense. Rather, it removed a device that looked something like a flashlight from its harness and pointed it at an open space on the capsule's wall. A schematic of the colony ship appeared.

"I don't know if my spectrum selection suits your visual range," Giant said apologetically. "Please tell me if you don't see four distinct wavelengths in the projection."

"Green, blue, black and red," Joe reported.

"It's fine." Paul nodded, but Beowulf shook his head in disgust. He only saw two colors, and the high-pitched squeal the capsule was making in the tube track was beginning to give him a headache. However, it was his first field engineering trip and he didn't want to start whining.

"Excellent," Giant said, the scratchy mechanical voice conveying the impression of a presenter at a lecture. "The black layer represents the infrastructure of the ship that is relatively sound, primarily structural members with sufficiently long operational lives to be considered unaffected by the passage of time." He manipulated a control on the projector and the black layer separated itself from the three-dimensional image and slid off to the side.

"The green layer represents infrastructure and equipment that is currently maintained at a satisfactory level, such as ceiling lights, ducting for temperature control and ventilation, plumbing for the ag decks, hydroponic farms, kitchens and bathrooms. The moving green shapes are mechanicals that are fully operational."

"Uh oh," Joe muttered, when Giant caused the green layer to slide off to the other side of the main projection. It was clear that a large proportion of the ship's systems were in trouble.

"The blue layer shows the parts of the ship for which maintenance is scheduled. In some cases, we simply haven't had the time as we concentrate resources on maintaining life-support systems for the ship's company. In other cases, we are in the process of fabricating the required parts, or we're waiting for the opportunity to obtain replacements, such as the main pile."

"Uh oh," Paul echoed Joe. The Zarent slid the blue layer off the schematic, leaving just the red. Judging by eye, it looked like approximately a fifth of the colony ship's equipment was in a critical state, including the service lift they were riding in.

"You see the problem," Giant said, causing the green, black and blue layers to disappear, and expanding the red into the vacated space. "This layer shows the systems which are, for lack of a more technical term, worn out. We keep them going on a break-fix basis, patching and jury-rigging, but no amount of maintenance or repair parts can make them new again. The Koffern and the cluster of Drazen colony ships forming this habitat are in average condition for the mob, primarily because they were built to last."

"I'm glad I don't have your job," Joe declared. "I guess the Wanderers must work harder at keeping things together than they let on."

The Zarent rose up and emitted a series of loud clicks again, a greater quantity than previously. Beowulf sank to the floor and put his paws over his ears.

"You are so funny!" Giant exclaimed. "My friends will buy me many rounds of Slurish for repeating your words. The Drazens on this ship are better than some of the Wanderers at cleaning up after themselves, and we even had a young woman helping with the planting last cycle, though she has abandoned the mob for work on Union Station. I was sorry to see her go, but there is too much social pressure on the Wanderers who don't fit in for the ambitious ones to stay here."

"Wait a second," Paul said, puzzled by the Zarent's explanation. "Why do you keep referring to the Wanderers as if you aren't a part of them?"

"Ah, I understand your confusion," Giant replied, settling back onto the floor. "It is true we are as much a part of the Wanderers as any of the other species represented in the mob, perhaps even more so. You see, my people were genetically engineered to serve the original Wanderers some tens of millions of years ago. We Zarents were a parting gift to the first mob from the Farlings, and although we have long since exceeded our original design specifications, we still exist to serve. Without us, the Wanderer mobs would simply fall apart."

"Are you, uh, free to leave if the work doesn't suit you?" Joe asked. Twenty years ago he would have asked outright if the Zarents were slaves, but marriage to the EarthCent ambassador had taught him a degree of diplomacy.

"Where would we go?" Giant asked in response. "You'll see that the core of the ship is given over to us entirely. We sleep in Zero-G along the axis of rotation, and we don't work on the high-gravity decks for more than a few hours at a time. Our bodies were designed for space construction and ship maintenance, and although our origins are artificial in nature, we have evolved to fit our niche."

"Speaking of gravity, I'd say it's dropping fast." Paul raised his arms and ventured a small bounce. It was a good thing he had his hands above his head because he was lighter than he expected, bouncing off the ceiling of the lift tube capsule, and again off the floor. On his second trip to the ceiling, he used his arms as shock absorbers, and gave the barest push back down, landing with his knees bent and straightening slowly.

"Be careful, boy," Joe instructed Beowulf. "I know how you hate getting upside down."

Beowulf, who had watched Paul's display through one eye squinted half shut, turned his head away in disgust. If he had known where the lift tube was heading, he would have stayed on the outermost deck catching meat scraps. Now, the pieces that he had ingested were refusing to sit properly in his stomach, and he felt the need to keep swallowing.

Joe rooted around in his rucksack and passed Paul a set of four modified magnetic cleats. The younger man crouched down and began strapping them around the dog's paws, pulling the friction belt tight on each. Beowulf remembered the utility of the cleats and endured the shoeing in stoic silence, but in his imagination, he was hatching a plot to weld the Nova to the deck in Mac's Bones and put an end to this traveling foolishness.

128

"Here we are," Giant announced, as the capsule came to a sudden halt and the door slid open. "You are welcome to use the webbing, but I'm afraid your four-legged friend would have difficulty navigating it."

The Zarent leapt from the door to an overhead mesh of cables, his unicycle grasped in a trailing appendage. The arrangement of the taut wires reminded Joe of the blueprints he had once seen for a rigid lighter-than-air craft that was deemed acceptable on some of the tech-ban worlds. In fact, if somebody had sewn a skin around the webbing, they would have ended up with something that looked very much like a dirigible, stretched through the core of the Drazen colony ship.

Joe and Paul switched on the magnetic cleats of their work boots and stepped out onto the innermost deck. The ship was spinning fast enough that even this close to the axis of rotation, they experienced an effective weight of a few pounds, but it was much easier to walk with the drag of the cleats than to try to slide along without bouncing. Beowulf rose gingerly and followed, finding that his stomach felt better when he was on his feet.

Moving fluidly overhead, Giant led them to the humming heart of the Drazen-engineered vessel. The pile produced power for everything but the ship's jump engines, which were unneeded in its current role as a habitat in a mob with tunneling escorts. The pile glowed a subdued red, and the hum warbled around the central frequency.

"I'm no expert on Drazen piles, and I've never seen one this big in person before, but it sounds a little off to me," Joe said. "Do you have the recent telemetry for the lasers and the magnetic bottle?"

"Certainly," Giant replied, removing the projector from his belt and bringing a bunch of wavy lines to life on the outer wall of the pile containment structure. "I haven't passed my level eight exam yet, but I believe the problem is with either the windings or the cores. We've upgraded the original controllers with Sharf differential current correction, but the fields refuse to remain stable."

"Hmm," Joe grunted, studying the waveforms. "Paul?"

"It looks to me like physical degradation," Paul said. "Maybe some of the elements still have life left in them, but by the time you tear the whole thing apart for rewinding, you've spent more than a new factory pile would cost. And the labor for a rebuild would run into weeks, which is a long time to run on backups."

"Our backup capacity for maintaining life support and sufficient light to prevent crop failure is approximately a hundred and forty hours," Giant interjected.

Beowulf ignored the conversation and concentrated on the hum from the pile, concluding that the excursions from the mean harmonic were growing. He barked once to get everybody's attention, pointed at the pile with one massive paw, and shook his head in the negative. Then he turned and trotted back to the lift tube.

"Well, there you have it," Joe declared. "I really don't know whether it's good for another year or another century, but it's way beyond the design life for the series and it's pretty far outside the safety specs. I suppose if it fails underway, you can always shut down and transfer to one of the other habitats, since you all seem to be crewed well below capacity. I sure wouldn't send it off alone on a colony mission."

"That is our assessment as well," the Zarent said. "Please inform the Drazen ambassador and the Union Station administration that Koffern has been declared unsafe to travel until the new pile is installed."

Thirteen

"Live, from the Grenouthian soundstage on Union Station. It's Species Wars!"

The audience roared and stamped their feet. Kelly stood stunned at the sudden name change to her show, wondering for a second if all of the high-tech gear on the set had caused her implant to glitch. Then a hologram showing an axe crossed with a plasma weapon appeared floating over the set, and she knew something had gone badly wrong.

Mr. Clavitts ran out onto the stage, dressed in a getup that made him look like a deranged leprechaun with a glandular problem, and took a theatrical bow. The Grenouthian prop staff had fixed him up with a scepter and instructed him to speak into it, even though all of the show's audio was actually captured by microphone arrays that could follow a buzzing fly through the room without a fluctuation in volume. Kelly understood now why the Grenouthian producer had drawn her aside for an urgent conference about nothing that had dragged on for two hours before the start of the show. The bunnies had changed it all on her!

"Welcome to the first broadcast of Species Wars. I'm your host, Doug Clavitts, and we're going to start right off selecting contestants from our studio audience." He paused and swept an arc over the audience with the scepter, the end of which now glowed brightly and cast a wide beam of red light. Invisible makeup on the foreheads of several aliens in the audience fluoresced when the red light illuminated them. Spotters quickly approached the marked sentients and ushered them to the back of the stage, where they were met by an assistant director wielding a bonded legal tab.

"The mark of Cain," Clavitts intoned into the scepter, employing an unnaturally low voice that sounded like it was emanating from a tomb. "Earth's pre-history collides with the tunnel network. While our contestants are being briefed, I'll explain the selection process. As our studio audience arrived today, they were asked to complete questionnaires in which we tested their knowledge of alien cultures and their feelings about interspecies cooperation."

Kelly relaxed a little on hearing they hadn't dispensed with the questionnaires. It had taken her weeks of working with Libby to come up with a customized list of questions for each species that would be relevant for their frame of reference. The idea was to select contestants who were naturally sympathetic to good interspecies relations, but who also held preconceptions about some of their traditional rivals that could be dispelled on the live holo-cast.

When the Grenouthian producer had received Kelly's final proposal, he'd gone wild over it, and the network had rushed the show into production much faster than Kelly had ever thought possible. She could see now that she should have listened to Aisha's advice about retaining an entertainment attorney, but maybe the name change and the weird emblem were just a come-on to attract viewers. After all, what did she know about show business? She heard the audience burst into wild cheers, and started paying attention again.

"I'm glad you all approve," Doug concluded, making Kelly wonder what she had missed while lost in her thoughts. She'd have to ask Libby to play it back for her during the first commercial break.

The eight contestants, each from a different species, emerged onto the stage simultaneously and seated themselves in pre-assigned pairs. Somehow, the Grenouthians had gotten it all backwards, seating individuals from feuding species together. The Dollnick was paired with the Frunge, the Horten with the Drazen, and the Vergallian with the human. Only the Grenouthian and the Verlock were on nominally good terms, and that was mainly because they had both been around too long to hold a grudge when business was involved.

"Before we move on to the questions, how about a little exercise in team building?" Clavitts asked, winking at the studio audience. "Who wants to volunteer for a bonus point?"

Kelly had worked with Aisha to prepare team building exercises for all of the possible alien pairings, though she hadn't planned to do any of them live. They just weren't that interesting, like coloring in pictures together and sharing water from a pitcher. It was kid stuff, really, which was the reason Kelly had chosen them. She didn't want the team building exercises to turn into a competition in their own right.

"I'll do it, Doug," the human contestant called out.

"It takes two to tango, Mr. uh, Scar," Clavitts responded, approaching the pair of contestants. "Is the lovely lady on board with this?"

The human and the Vergallian were indeed an odd pairing. The young man, somewhere in his early twenties by Kelly's estimate, looked like he had spent his youth running the corridors, probably involved in the low-level scams and questionable recreational activities that passed for crime on Union Station. The Vergallian was attractive, but she looked like a defective copy of the upper caste women who rotated rapidly through the ambassadorial posts and functioned as the royalty in the Empire of a Hundred Worlds.

"Tell me about the exercise and I'll tell you if I'm on board, Human," the Vergallian replied.

The host approached the pair and whispered rapidly to each one in turn before stepping to the side. The young man rolled up his sleeves to display his amateurish tattoos and stepped out from behind the little desk-like stand provided for each pair of contestants. The Vergallian woman followed and positioned herself behind him.

"For a point then," Clavitts said, and snapped his fingers. A bunny in the wings began rapidly patting his belly, producing a bass version of a drum roll. "Three, two, one!"

The human leaned backwards, looked puzzled, and lost his balance. When he realized that his partner wouldn't be catching him, he got his arms back, but it was too late to really soften the impact that much, and he hit with a thud.

The Vergallian stood aside with her hands spread, a wicked smile on her face, and said, "Oops."

"Way to take one for the team," Clavitts proclaimed, as the audience erupted in laughter. "I think we can give you a point for trying. Now, on to the first question, this one for the Grenouthian and the Verlock. If it weren't for the Stryx rules, which species on the tunnel network would you attack first?"

Kelly actually yelled, "Hey!" out loud this time, but nobody heard over the roar of the studio audience. The question was supposed to be, "If the Stryx suddenly abandoned the tunnel network, what species would you turn to first to begin building an alliance to fill the gap?"

The Grenouthian and the Verlock looked at each other questioningly, and then the giant bunny nodded and said, "Each other?"

"Correct!" Clavitts yelled, reading rapidly from prompts appearing on his heads-up display "As two of the oldest and wealthiest species on the tunnel network, getting the jump on your main rival could make all of the difference. I'll take that answer for both of you and award two points." The host glanced at the Grenouthian director and saw him counting down. "We're going to take a quick commercial break, and then we'll be back with the rest of the first round."

Kelly tried yelling at the director to get his attention, but he was around the other side of the stage, and the whole area was a mass of burly bunnies running this way and that. She recalled that the first break was only forty-six seconds or whatever the standard spot was on the Grenouthian network, so she forced herself to calm down and called for help.

"Libby? They've turned my show into a bad joke. Can you replay for me what Mr. Clavitts said while the assistant director was briefing the contestants backstage?"

"I'm sorry to hear about the show, Kelly," Libby answered immediately. "It doesn't look like something you would be involved in at all. Here's the replay you requested, starting thirty seconds back."

"As our studio audience arrived today, they were asked to complete questionnaires in which we tested their knowledge level of alien cultures and their feelings about interspecies cooperation. From those questionnaires, we selected the individuals who scored the worst on both factual knowledge and empathy. After all, if it's warm fuzzy feelings you want, you can watch 'Let's Make Friends' every day on this network. And now, to war!"

Kelly gnashed her teeth and looked for the Grenouthian director, who was counting back in from the commercial break. She began working her way around the set, muttering under her breath as Clavitts started in again with the banter. It was only her sense of propriety as the EarthCent Ambassador that held her back from running onto the stage and declaring that her show had been hijacked.

"It's just the Grenouthian approach to entertainment," Libby said through Kelly's implant, trying to calm her friend. "I know you don't watch many holo-casts yourself, but other than the documentaries and sports, confrontational-type live shows are very popular. Think of it as a harmless outlet for the bottled-up aggression that we don't allow on the tunnel network."

"But they're joking about war like it's some kind of game!" Kelly subvoced back. "And they're doing it under the EarthCent brand." She came to a halt, blocked by the broad backsides of a row of large bunnies she couldn't push past. "What time is it on Earth? Can you put me through to the President? I have to warn him."

"Secure channel to EarthCent headquarters opened," Libby reported. "The president isn't available, but a Hildy Greuen would like to speak with you."

"Put her on," Kelly groaned, recognizing the name of EarthCent's new branding consultant. She wondered if being an ambassador gave her diplomatic immunity against lawsuits initiated by her own employers.

"Great show!" Hildy exclaimed. "I know you must be busy with a million things, but try to make sure Mr. Clavitts has our script for the product placement, and I look forward to meeting you in person sometime. Can I give the president a message for you?"

"Uh, no, that's alright," Kelly subvoced. "The, er, show isn't exactly what I planned. You're not worried about EarthCent's brand suffering?"

"First viewers, then content," the marketing expert replied. "We can't sell them on peace and cooperation if we can't get them to watch. Oh, did you see that? The guy with the four arms looks like he's going to kill somebody. I'm going to let you go because I know how much these calls cost."

"Nice talking to you," Kelly subvoced to dead air. Now she knew that at least one of the Earth networks had picked up the tunneling feed from the Stryx and were broadcasting live, so even if she'd reached the president, there was no way to stop people from seeing it. A small gap appeared in the crowd of Grenouthians in front of her, and she squeezed between a couple of soft bellies, emerging in the clear.

"I always heard that the Drazens and the Hortens had it in for each other, but I never thought I'd see mature sentients let a vendetta get in the way of a great deal," Clavitts remarked, scratching his head in his folksy way. "Each of you had half of the answer on your heads-up display, so all you had to do was put it together and you would have won the first round. Weren't you paying attention when we assigned the teams?"

"Better the station should fall into a black hole than I should help a Drazen," the Horten remarked scornfully.

"The day a Horten can do anything to help a Drazen is the day I choke myself with my own tentacle," the Drazen responded, not even looking in his assigned partner's direction.

Clavitts caught Kelly's eye where she stood in the wings and shook his head. His own suggestion had been to rehearse the whole show using a script and actors, rather than going live with volunteers from the studio audience. Fortunately, he'd negotiated his own contract, and the Grenouthians were on the hook to pay him for a season even if the show closed on the first night.

"So the first round goes to our senior citizens, the Verlock and the Grenouthian," Clavitts continued, trying to sound upbeat. "When we come back after the commercial break, we'll be showing you some of the great Earth products the winners will be taking home, and then we'll move on to the direct questioning round. Don't touch that hologram!"

"What happened to the questions I prepared?" Kelly shouted at Clavitts, who was getting a quick repair job from the make-up artist. "It's supposed to be about cooperation and learning new things about each other, but you're making it into a war!"

"I'm just following instructions from the booth," Clavitts replied. "It never would have occurred to me to draw attention to the fact that the Dollnick was pretending to pick insects out of the Frunge's hair vines and eating them. It's like a bad school cafeteria up here."

"Fantastic!" the Grenouthian director proclaimed, coming up to Kelly's side, and pointing at the instantaneous ratings. "Two percent of the live audience for the first broadcast of a show may not make you rich in this galaxy, but you won't starve either."

"You've ruined it!" Kelly hissed venomously at the startled bunny. "I don't care about your stupid ratings. I wanted to help people."

138

"The producer made some last minute changes to try to pick up the energy," the director said nervously. "It's normal to feel this way about a new show, but you'll get used to it. Didn't you get the revisions?"

"I certainly didn't," Kelly responded angrily, as the director began counting down the commercial break. "What's next? A food fight?"

"And we're back," Clavitts declared, putting on his showman's smile. "Before we turn the questioning over to the contestants, let's see what they can win."

Clavitts swept an arm towards the side of the stage, which was the cue for an attractive young bunny who was related in some way to the producer to bring out a floater with the featured Earth exports. This week it was aged single malt Scotch in hand-blown glass bottles. The Frunge licked his lips and the Drazen looked interested for the first time.

"That's eighteen-year-old single malt, my friends," the host declared, glancing at some print scribbled on the palm of his hand and speaking rapidly. "Kissed by the ocean breeze, this Speyside single cask whiskey is just one of the wonderful products exported by Earth." He paused, shaking off an instruction from the booth and uttering the catch line decided on by the EarthCent marketing guru, "Just ask a human."

"Time for the lottery," the Grenouthian girl piped in a reedy voice. She extended to Clavitts a fishbowl that contained eight balls, one for each of the contestants on the show. The young bunny wasn't supposed to have any lines, but the producer in the booth had instructed her to take the container from the table and speak the four words, just to remind Clavitts who was boss.

"Right," Clavitts declared, casually reaching into the bowl. He pulled out a ball and dramatically threw it to the floor. There was a flash of light, and a hologram of the Vergallian contestant appeared, turned about, and walked over to the real Vergallian, where the two merged. It was a new effect that the producer had recommended trying, and the Grenouthian crew all breathed a sigh of relief when it came off properly.

"Who do you choose to question?" Clavitts asked the Vergallian woman.

"The Drazen," she replied. In accordance with the assistant director's hastily imparted instructions before the show, she pointed dramatically at her choice. "For myself and for all of the Vergallian women, I want to know why Drazen men think they're attractive?"

The studio audience stomped their feet, whistled in derision, laughed and howled. Kelly looked at the director in horror, who pointed at the instantaneous ratings. They had just spiked up and were now climbing steadily.

Clavitts turned reluctantly to the Drazen, attempting to maintain a cheery smile. The Drazen's tentacle was sticking up like an angry club behind his head, and Kelly couldn't believe that his glare didn't vaporize the Vergallian woman where she stood.

"Your answer, sir?" the host prompted, the first time in the show he had addressed anyone formally.

"Well, we didn't always think so," the Drazen replied icily. "It wasn't until we joined the tunnel network and were able to compare our score cards with males of other species that we found ourselves on top, so to speak."

Kelly cringed and looked to Joe in the audience for support, but he was busy explaining something to Dorothy. The director's eyes were glued to the ratings meter, and Clavitts was starting to look like he'd been trapped in a bad barter. He reached back into the bowl helpfully proffered by the assistant, and flung a new ball to the floor. A hologram of the Drazen stepped out of the flash and walked directly to its enraged source.

"And who do you..." Clavitts began to ask, but the Drazen cut him off sharply.

"Vergallian! Under the rules of the show, I demand a 'Yes' or a 'No' answer. Have you already spent over a hundred thousand creds on cosmetic surgery in your attempt to pass as upper caste?"

"That's a trap question, there's no right answer," she protested vehemently, baring her nearly perfect teeth. "I demand he withdraws it!"

"There's a first time for everything!" the Drazen cried, mugging for the camera. The Vergallian realized she'd been tricked into a double entendre, whipped a dagger out of her boot and hurled it at the Drazen's head. It shattered the mirror which the Grenouthian production crew had introduced to make the holo-stunts work. She grabbed the dagger from the other boot and her eyes searched the stage for the flesh-and-blood Drazen, who had wisely ducked out of sight.

"We'll be right back after a commercial break," Clavitts shouted over the crowd noise. The director gave the all-clear, and a crew rushed on stage with a new mirror. The assistant director, who had collected signed disclaimers from the contestants backstage, leapt in front of the Vergallian woman and began a hurried explanation of the small print. Before the mirror was replaced, she had accepted a sedative and returned to her seat.

"This is a disaster," Kelly shouted at the director. "I won't have anything to do with it."

"We're up to an eight share!" the director shouted back, pointing at the display. "We're a hit."

"It's a nightmare and I'm leaving," she proclaimed. Nightmare?

Kelly began to pinch herself energetically, and after that failed, seized a bottle of water and poured it over her own head. As Clavitts started in again with a new question, Joe appeared out of nowhere and grabbed her arm.

"Joe, I had the worst nightmare yet," she sobbed, focusing thankfully on his face. "The bunnies turned my show into a—why are we still standing in the studio?"

"It's not a nightmare, Kelly," Joe said, getting hold of both of her hands and pulling her towards the exit. "Dorothy's waiting for us in the corridor. I think we'd better go home."

Fourteen

"Stop following me!" Samuel demanded. He turned around and faced the little Vergallian girl who had been dogging his footsteps in Mac's Bones all morning. Both children had finished their recent rotation in the cast of LMF, and Aisha had placed her foundling in Libby's kindergarten, with Kelly's son. Banger, the young Stryx who was Samuel's work-play assignment, hovered uncertainly at the boy's side. Ailia looked like she was about to burst into tears.

"Sh'eeda insrook," she said pathetically. Ailia wished she could persuade Aisha to bring her to work every day. The Vergallian girl had promised the human woman that she knew how to sit quietly and stay out of the way. It was what she'd been doing for the last two years, but the younger Mrs. McAllister had insisted she remain home and play. Ailia still had trouble understanding all of the different names the humans went by, and it seemed crazy to have two Mrs. McAllisters living in the same home.

"Speak English!" Samuel ordered peremptorily. Then he turned to Banger and asked, "What did she say?"

"Be my friend," Banger rasped in his developing artificial voice. "I think we should."

"Zhshint!" Samuel declared, one of the Vergallian words for "no" he had picked up. It seemed to him that the language had too many words for everything, another fact the boy held against the new guest in their home, who also monopolized his father's attention with all of her questions. Kelly had explained to Samuel that Joe knew the Vergallian language from a previous job, though she wouldn't go into detail about it, and that the girl was alone in the galaxy and needed their help.

Ailia sat down on the deck and pouted, though she felt better since the boy had used the soft form of "no" that actually meant something closer to the positive form of "maybe," with the intent of "no moving towards yes," implied by the intonation.

Beowulf flopped on the floor beside the girl and eyed her cautiously. He remembered being strongly biased against Vergallians, but Joe, Woojin and Clive all seemed to like the little girl, so he was willing to suspend judgment for the time being. The girl smelled tired to him, and even without the emotional trauma of her nurse abandoning her, she was having trouble adapting to the twenty-four-hour day the humans maintained. Beowulf nudged her with his massive head and rolled his eyes up towards his back. Did she want a ride?

Samuel turned about abruptly and set off for the training area, where an advanced group of EarthCent Intelligence recruits were getting an introduction to techban combat from Joe and Woojin. Banger hesitated for a moment, dipped in apology, and then set off after his human friend.

Ailia looked at the hound, trying to read his intent. Her people were all horsemen, and the mother she could barely remember had first set her on a pony on her third birthday. But she'd never ridden alone, and she didn't see a saddle or guiding leads on Beowulf. Still, she could feel him willing her to try, so she gently climbed onto his back while he sprawled on the floor, and took a hold of the loose fur and skin behind his neck.

Beowulf rose slowly, exercising more caution than he'd ever employed before in his young life. He was accustomed to carrying loads for Joe in his mouth or in saddle bags, and sometimes Aisha took him to the Shuk when she was stocking up on supplies, but he wasn't sure he'd be able to keep the girl balanced. Fortunately, riding must have been in her genes, because she kept her seat without even pulling on his hair. He followed Samuel and Banger at a gentle walk.

"Now, let's say he's coming at me with a knife," Woojin said to the trainees. He slipped the dagger from his belt sheath and tossed it to Joe, who caught it by the bone handle. The former mercenary officer had no regrets about leaving his fighting days behind, but he enjoyed the challenge of teaching basic self-defense to the variety of types that EarthCent Intelligence attracted, and it helped establish trust with the agents heading into the field.

"Not the knife," Joe grumbled. He looked at the weapon sourly. Charging Woojin with a knife always ended in a wrist-manipulation that left him sore for days, no matter how gentle his friend tried to be. "Hey, look behind you, Wooj. It's the Vergallian girl riding Beowulf!"

Woojin shook his head sadly at Joe for even trying such a lame trick. For some reason, the trainees all went along with it, pointing and smiling at something behind him. Out of the corner of his eye, he saw Samuel and Banger angling past the training area on their way to Dring's.

Joe saw his friend's attention shift and immediately attacked. A second later, Woojin was holding Joe's wrist locked, demonstrating the twist and flip in slow motion.

After the initial demonstration, Woojin directed the trainees to pair up and practice the move with their rubber knives. When he finally gave in to curiosity and looked over his shoulder, he saw that Ailia was riding erect on Beowulf's back, following the boy and the young Stryx.

"First time in my life that trick should have worked and you refused to look," Joe complained, rubbing his wrist. "I'm proud of the way Beowulf is helping the girl. I wish my boy was a little gentler with her."

"Never had any kids of my own, but I'd say they're both doing fine," Woojin reassured him. "The fact she's still following him around must mean he's doing something right."

Samuel and Banger reached the mound of scrap that shielded Dring's area from the rest of Mac's Bones and headed into the camouflaged tunnel. A minute later, Joe and Woojin saw Ailia duck her head, and the second pair disappeared. The instructors turned back to their trainees, who were doing their best not to poke each other's eyes out with the rubber daggers.

"You can't come in without Dring's permission," Samuel said, holding up a hand to stop the girl and the dog when they emerged from the tunnel. Ailia caught the gist of his meaning, but Beowulf just shook his head at the boy and continued towards the gravity surfer at a sedate pace. Samuel stamped after them in annoyance.

"I'm sure Dring will welcome them if he's here," Banger said, which gave his friend a new idea.

"Nobody's home," Samuel declared, coming to a halt. "Me and Banger are going back."

The girl twisted cautiously on Beowulf's back and asked, "D'neenah?"

"Zhshint," Samuel replied dismissively, unconsciously getting the tone just right to express, "probably not."

"Pa'ash," Dring declared, coming around the corner from his vegetable garden. The Maker had developed into an epicure of carrots, and had bought the plot of sandy soil and the box used to contain it after the caber tossing competition. He claimed his produce tasted better than the Shuk-bought vegetables, and supplied the McAllisters with his surplus.

"You speak Vergallian?" Samuel asked in surprise, not having figured out yet that he was beginning to learn it himself. "Now everybody is going to know what she's saying except for me."

"You're too young for implants, Samuel, and you have Banger to translate the words you miss. But your mother told me you might be bringing your new friend by one day, and I have something for her that will help." Dring spoke first in English and then repeated himself in Vergallian. "Would you like to come in?"

The friendly shape-shifter ushered the children and the dog into the gravity surfer and made directly for the bench next to the little pond. The top of the bench tilted up as he approached, and the children saw that it covered a narrow storage box. Dring rooted around for a moment before coming up with an odd flesh-colored device that looked a little like a lower jaw without the teeth.

"T'inda," he said, extending it towards the girl. "A gift," he repeated for Samuel's benefit.

Beowulf lowered himself carefully onto his belly, as if he had been a camel and not a war dog in his previous life. Ailia clambered off, scratched him fondly behind his ears in thanks, and then approached Dring, who fit the device over her ear.

"It's a language trainer for species with external ears," he explained. "I've set it to Vergallian, so it will start by translating almost everything you hear, but as you use English, it will learn the words you know and only offer translation if you tap it on the back there."

Ailia's tired face lit up with joy when she realized the device would do something similar to the in-ear plugs the Grenouthians had supplied to the child actors on the LMF set. Aisha had asked to borrow or buy one of the ear plugs from the Grenouthians, but they explained that it was only a receiver, and that the translations the children heard during the show originated from the booth.

"Now I'll understand everything you say," she declared, turning to Samuel with shining eyes.

"What?" the boy said, having missed the words in the middle of her sentence. While Banger translated for him, Dring rummaged around in his bench-box and brought out another ear cuff.

"T'inda," he said, extending it to Samuel. "I've set this one to translate Vergallian to English. You might offer to share it with Aisha."

"Who cares what a girl says," the boy bluffed, turning his head so Dring could fit the ear cuff for him. Then he remembered that part of his job was teaching Banger good human manners, so he added, "Thank you," and then stuck out his tongue at Ailia.

"Now that we all understand each other, shall we play a game?" Dring asked.

The youngsters agreed enthusiastically, including Ailia, whose fatigue had been washed away by the doggy-back ride and the language-teaching device.

"Why don't we all sit down in a circle," Dring continued, settling back a bit on his haunches. He never sat in

148

chairs on account of his tail, which remained with him through the various shapes he assumed. Samuel kept Banger between himself and the Vergallian girl. "I know a game called 'Memory,' and the rules are very easy. Shall we play it?"

"Who goes first?" Samuel asked, arriving immediately at the heart of the matter.

"Hmm, that's a good question," Dring replied. "I believe it goes, Human, Vergallian, Stryx, Huravian, Maker. Does that sound right?"

Beowulf looked suspicious about the order, but he held his peace, and Dring continued.

"Each player gets to ask the person two places to their right a question about something they remember, and that person has to answer. Are you ready?"

All of the sentients, with the exception of Dring, surreptitiously counted two spaces to their right to see who they would get to quiz. Beowulf and Banger also counted two back the other way to see who would be asking them questions. Beowulf broke into a large doggy smile.

Samuel looked at the dog distrustfully. After all, Beowulf had practically gone over to the enemy by giving Ailia a ride. Then he thought of something.

"Beowulf," Samuel said. "Do you remember the flyer Grandpa sent me?"

Beowulf nodded in the affirmative. How could he forget the foam stunt plane that seemed to attack him from behind no matter which direction the boy threw it. Sneaky, that's what the thing was. If it hadn't been a present, the dog would have chewed it to pieces. Fortunately, the boy had lost sight of it on one throw, and the plane skidded under the ice harvester before rising up to wedge itself behind the old escape hatch. Samuel had never found it.

"Do you know where it is?" the boy asked hopefully.

Beowulf hedged for a minute, licking the side of his nose. He knew where it was the last time he looked, but it was entirely possible somebody had moved it since then, in which case he didn't know where it was. He glanced over at Dring, who gave him a stern look. The dog sighed heavily and nodded again.

"Can I have it back? I promise not to lose it again."

Not the promise Beowulf was hoping for, but he got up and trotted off to retrieve the thing. Maybe if they were still playing when he got back, he could sneak into a different spot and ask Dring a question. He didn't want to waste a memory question on Banger, whom he could ask anytime.

"Now it's your turn, young lady," Dring said to the Vergallian girl. "What do you want to ask Samuel?"

Ailia didn't hesitate for a second.

"Do you remember on the show when we shared the crayons, and you said that's what friends do?" she asked eagerly.

"That was for the show," Samuel said dismissively, looking at the floor. "I was just acting."

"Oh," Ailia said, and her perfect little face started to crumple. She had a horrible thought. What if Aisha and the rest of the McAllisters were just acting about liking her?

Banger poked his friend with his pincer and pointed at the girl, who was beginning to cry.

"I mean, we all act on the show, but I guess we're friends at home, sort-of." It was a major concession for the boy.

"Really?" Ailia asked in English, one of the words she'd picked up from Dorothy.

"I guess," Samuel reiterated.

The girl tapped her ear cuff, which translated the phrase into, "positive assumption with a high degree of certitude." Although the high caste Vergallians matured physically at about half the rate of humans, it was due to the fact that their bodies invested so much more energy in developing their cognitive skills in their early years, especially useful for the highly nuanced language. She stopped crying and smiled happily.

"Now you get to ask me a memory question, young Stryx," Dring said. He never would have thought of trying to evoke Samuel's sympathy if he hadn't read through Kelly's collection of children's books. They offered a much better operating manual for the human psyche than the medical books he'd also studied.

"When Metoo was High Priest of the Kasilians, did he really make the decisions, or were you there to tell him what to do?" Banger asked. The young Stryx in Libby's experimental school all looked up to Jeeves and Metoo as heroes, but there was some debate over how much they were being advised by the older Stryx, and in Metoo's case, by the Maker as well.

"Metoo would often ask me to help him explain things to the Kasilians, but as far as I know, he made his own decisions," Dring replied. "The Kasilians were quite capable of taking care of themselves, of course, once Metoo made the decision for them to abandon their home world."

"Thank you," Banger said, applying his recent lesson from Samuel.

"Since Beowulf isn't back yet, I'll go ahead with my turn and ask Ailia a question," Dring said. "What is your happiest memory since coming to Union Station?"

"I have two," the girl replied. "When the Mrs. McAllisters said I was going to live in their home, and just now, when Samuel said that we were friends as a positive assumption with a high degree of certitude."

Samuel tapped his ear cuff after the flood of Vergallian, and heard, "when Samuel said that we were friends, he guessed." He looked at Ailia, blushed, and looked at the floor. She'd never be as good as Banger or a little boy, but at least she wasn't as bossy as Dorothy and Mist.

Beowulf came trotting back to Dring's, the foam plane held gently in his mouth. It had taken him a number of tries to determine that by repositioning the weight in the slot, the plane would glide straight rather than looping. He added an "accidental" crimp with his canines to lock the weight in place. It would be much more fun watching the boy chasing the plane than craning his own head around and waiting for a surprise attack from behind.

Fifteen

"I can't tell you how much I appreciate your coming," Kelly said to Shaina. The two women had met by appointment in the hallway outside the waiting room of the Thark arbitrator, and entered together. "If only you'd been on the station when I signed the contract, I know we wouldn't be here today."

"I'm sure you've been hearing this from everybody, but you really shouldn't have signed a Grenouthian contract without legal representation," Shaina replied, trying not to sound overly critical. "You have to think of the entertainment industry as a law office with a subsidiary that does show business. And how come you didn't ask Libby for help?"

"I don't know," Kelly responded. "No, that's not true, I do know. I wanted to show everybody that I could handle it myself."

"Well, you did make them agree to binding arbitration on Union Station," Shaina said. "That was smart. If you had signed the original contract you showed me, the governing law and the jurisdiction were both on the Grenouthian home world. I've heard they have a backlog of decades, and you have to be resident during the waiting period or your case is dismissed."

"I'm not a complete idiot," Kelly muttered, though as it happened, Joe had warned her about jurisdiction and

153

governing law in contracts before she went to meet the Grenouthian producer the first time. She glanced at the faux mechanical wristwatch Shaina had helped her buy when they first met in the Shuk. "I wonder where the producer is. It's almost time."

The door to the arbitration chambers slid open, and a casually dressed Drazen woman emerged with a smile that practically split her face in two. A few seconds later, Bork followed her, looking like he'd been served a bowl of dirt for breakfast and told to like it. The Thark arbitrator stuck his head out, nodded at Kelly, noted that the Grenouthians hadn't arrived yet, and withdrew.

"Bork!" Kelly said loudly, as the Drazen walked right past without seeing her. "Am I wearing an invisibility projector or something?"

The Drazen ambassador jerked his head around and made a conscious effort to become aware of his surroundings.

"My apologies, Ambassador," he said formally. "I just received a final decision from the arbitrator, tens of millions of creds of liability."

"That's terrible," Kelly said in sympathy. "Who was that woman?"

"A Wanderer attorney, the worst kind," Bork replied, collapsing into the seat next to Kelly. "She produced a contract signed by one of my predecessors many thousands of years ago, promising to replace the piles on all of the Drazen colony ships in their habitat cluster when the first one failed. There was a recall out on that model of colony ship at the time, which the Wanderers agreed to forfeit, since it involved the terraforming equipment they didn't use. In return, the Drazen ambassador, acting for the shipyard, agreed to the insane warranty deal for the piles.

154

Everybody knows the Wanderers run these ships until they fall apart."

"And what did the arbitrator say?" Shaina asked.

"That I didn't have a tentacle to hang from," Bork groaned. "The contract was clear, and it even specified Thark arbitration for any difficulties. Despite the fact that it was a ridiculously bad deal signed by a first-year ambassador who neither consulted with the home office nor filed the contract in the embassy system, it's valid. The Thark had it on record, both in their own system and with the Stryx. If Ambassador Fadok hadn't died thousands of years ago, and if his family hadn't sold the shipyard—well, that's all vacuum under the keel, now."

"Joe said something to me about going out to look at a pile for you," Kelly said. "Did he do something wrong?"

"No, it's not his fault," Bork replied. "In fact, it's a miracle the things held up as long as they have. I'm just sorry the Zarents couldn't keep it humming until somebody else was the Drazen ambassador." Having an audience for his complaints helped, and Bork began to perk up, at which point it dawned on him that the humans weren't hanging out in the arbitrator's waiting room for no reason. "May I ask what the two of you are doing here?"

"It's my contract with the Grenouthians," Kelly explained. "The show they're doing is a travesty. They stole my ideas and did the exact opposite, right down the line. They're even using the questionnaires I prepared to pick the most immature and xenophobic audience members for contestants, the first ones I would have screened out."

"Do you have the contract with you?" Bork asked. Shaina handed over her tab, and the Drazen ambassador rapidly paged through it, recording images through his implant. Then he gazed blankly at the far wall while reading the translation on his heads-up display.

"Not good," he muttered. "No, not good at all. Oh, no. They're still including that clause in contracts? I thought the Stryx banned it. No, no, ugh. I'm sorry Kelly. I've signed plenty of Grenouthian contracts over the years for my work in the immersives and I'm afraid they gave you the standard model, which is to say, the version they wish they could get everybody to sign. But here, the one thing you have going for you is the royalties. That's actually an above-market rate."

"I got that from Aisha," Kelly admitted. "She renegotiated a few months ago, or rather, her Thark counsel did, and the Grenouthians caved on royalties when I told them I saw her contract. I didn't get quite as much, but it was five times what they initially offered."

"That's how it is with contracts," Shaina said grimly. "When they're dealing with amateurs, they'll be flexible with the top line numbers, but they pretend that the rest of the language is carved in stone."

"The show is doing very well in the ratings," Bork mused. "If you're willing to give up some of those royalties, it's a nice bonus for them, so they may display a little flexibility. What is it you want?"

"I want my show back!" Kelly exclaimed. "They can keep all of the royalties, I don't care. I just don't want my name on their version, they may as well shoot the whole thing in an x-rated pirate's bar. It's bad enough that the host is human, but I talked to Mr. Clavitts and his contract is ironclad. When he signed, he was only worried that they would discontinue the show and dump him. Now he's stuck."

"Remember, you promised not to open your mouth in chambers if I came along." Shaina issued this stern warning to Kelly, and then turned to explain to Bork. "She's not very business savvy, but I think we can do better than just walking away. She really wanted to do something positive."

"If you're willing to give up the money, you might get the Grenouthians to agree to another show, but I wouldn't expect them to offer more than the use of a small studio and crew," Bork said. "The Grenouthians are overstaffed because every bunny and his cousin wants into the business, and they always have more than enough equipment. But there's still a huge difference between a show with a budget and those public service bits they use to fill bandwidth when nobody is watching."

The door to the corridor slid open and a string of Grenouthians filed in. Kelly recognized the producer, of course, but he appeared to be under instruction from his advocates not to acknowledge her.

"I've never seen such a scary bunch of bunnies," Shaina whispered to Kelly as the Grenouthians settled on the bench as far from the humans as possible. "Remember. Let me do the talking when we get inside."

The Thark arbitrator must have been monitoring the waiting room because the door to his chambers slid open a moment after the Grenouthians seated themselves. Perhaps making them get up as soon as they sat down was his revenge for their making him wait.

"Shall I join you, just to balance the sides a little?" Bork asked the EarthCent ambassador.

"Would you?" Kelly immediately felt better. She had tremendous confidence in Shaina's deal-making ability, but all of the Hadads were small people, and the Grenouthians were so large.

They entered the arbitrator's chambers and took their seats at the triangular table, with one of the Grenouthians forced to remain standing for lack of room on the bench. The Thark reserved one side of the equilateral triangle for himself, and his bench was plainly higher than the other two, since he managed to look down on all of the seated bunnies.

"I am activating the recorder now, making this arbitration session binding," the Thark warned them. "Any exchange including offer, acceptance and consideration, will be registered as a de facto modification to the current contract. Are you clear on the terms?"

"Yes," Shaina declared, her powerful alto voice always coming as a surprise to Kelly.

"Get on with it," the lead Grenouthian advocate grunted.

"I have reviewed your written arguments, a prima facie case of creator's regret. As the first step of the arbitration process, each party will give an oral summary of their position. This is to ensure that you are actually listening to each other." The Thark arbitrator leaned forward, bridged his hands under his chin in a picture of concentration, and nodded at the Grenouthian attorney.

"I would be derelict in my duty if I didn't begin by pointing out that the human's pouch is empty," the bunny stated. "However, as the contract does stipulate this arbitration process to settle any differences, we will play along."

"What did he mean about my pouch being empty?" Kelly subvoced to Bork on his private channel, not wanting to distract Shaina.

158

"It's the same as not having a tentacle to hang from," Bork subvoced back. "What's the human expression? A leg to stand on."

"I have prepared a few key excerpts from the contract," the Grenouthian continued. "May I patch into your display?"

The Thark inclined his head briefly in response.

"Here, I've circled it in red, and I'll read aloud, since that was your request." The advocate cleared his throat and then continued. "All final decisions about the content and production of the show, including the title, selection of contestants, questions, special effects, and action scenes, shall be made by the Director or the Producer assigned by the Grenouthian network. All artistic input from the Creator will be given due consideration, and the Director and Producer will make themselves available to meet with the Creator on the presentation of a written request, no more than six times per season."

"I've received no such request," the producer interrupted, and then wilted under the glare of his attorney.

"We could present further clauses that clearly delineate the roles and authority of the parties involved, but I don't want to waste the arbitrator's expensive time on an open-and-shut case," the scary bunny concluded in a bored voice.

The arbitrator showed no offense on hearing his time categorized as "expensive," and turned to Kelly's side of the table.

"Ambassador McAllister signed a contract, with the encouragement of the Grenouthian Ambassador, who received a point in the production as a finder's fee," Shaina stated to begin her presentation. "From the first day of discussions, Ambassador McAllister made clear that her goal was to create a show that would lead to better under-standing among species and increase the visibility of EarthCent and humanity. Our Grenouthian friends, knowingly and by pre-design, produced a show that is the mirror opposite of Ambassador McAllister's plan."

"Alleged pre-design," the Grenouthian objected.

"Objection noted, but you aren't trying a court case here," the Thark remarked.

"The resulting show is damaging to both Ambassador McAllister's diplomatic reputation, and to the EarthCent brand," Shaina continued. "We have turned to contract arbitration in hopes of settling our differences, but the contract does not indemnify the Grenouthians from inflicting reputational damage."

The Grenouthian producer made a derisive sound and began whispering to his legal representative. At first, the advocate looked annoyed, but then he began paying attention, and finally, he showed his lower teeth in amusement.

"If you choose to pursue damages, we will meet you in court," the bunny said smoothly. "Of course, we would be forced to present evidence of the ambassador's self-inflicted reputational damage over the years, which I understand is both well-documented and copious."

Kelly glowered at the Grenouthians, but from the mo-ment Shaina had told her about the damages gambit, she knew that they couldn't go to court for just that reason. From putting a young Stryx in a coma from emotional shock, to crying on the podium at an important interstellar conference, the ambassador had too many reputational skeletons in her closet to cast the first stone.

"Now, if we have the threats and counter-threats out of the way, let's hear what you hoped to accomplish by coming here and paying my exorbitant fees," the arbitrator stated. "Let's start with you this time," he added, nodding to Shaina.

"Ambassador McAllister requests that her name be removed from all credits and viewer guides related to Species Wars, and that she receive a broadcast slot and production support for the show she was originally contracted to produce," Shaina said succinctly.

The Grenouthian counsel turned his head sixty degrees to look directly at Shaina for the first time. He hadn't actually put much effort into preparing for the arbitration session since it was an obvious win for the network. But the producer had led him to believe that Kelly was demanding immediate cancellation of the hit show, something that the Grenouthians would never have done, even if the arbitrator found against them. What the little one had asked for sounded more like a negotiation.

"I request a few minutes to confer with my client," the giant bunny said. He turned back to the Thark, who as usual, merely inclined his head in response. The Grenouthians all rose and trooped out to the waiting room.

"I think it's going pretty well," Bork ventured, impressed with Shaina's nerve. His own arbitration session had been a disaster, mainly because the Wanderer representative had custom, practice, the law, and a contract registered by both the Tharks and the Stryx on her side. In retrospect, the Drazen ambassador wasn't sure why he had ever requested arbitration in the first place, because, as the Thark admitted, the fee was exorbitant. "If he mentions the royalties when they come back in, it means you have them by the belly fur."

"You're doing great," Kelly encouraged Shaina. "I would have been in tears by now."

"I wish you'd picked a fight with the Dollnicks," the small woman replied gloomily. "They're bigger and louder, but they really can't stand confrontations that don't fit into their hierarchical world view. The Grenouthians have been in this racket for millions of years and they hold all of the cards. If they agree to a change, it's because they know they'll be getting a better deal."

"I don't mean to eavesdrop, but you're paying for my time, so I may as well give you my opinion," the Thark spoke up unexpectedly. "I've worked as an arbitrator for over two hundred years now, and I've never seen a contract that, from a free market standpoint, wasn't a better deal for one side than the other. Good contracts are like good trades, with both sides getting something they want more than what they are giving in return."

"I know," Shaina admitted. "I just hate seeing the Grenouthians get what they want. They really did take advantage of her on the contract."

The Thark glanced at the door, reached in his pocket, and slid something across the triangular table to Kelly.

"I'm not really supposed to do this, but that's my sister's holo-cube, she represents artists in contract negotiations. It's quite a specialized field, especially when you consider the subsidiary rights for action figures, spin-offs and the like. Just tell her I sent you."

"Fifteen percent finder's fee to the brother," Bork subvoced to Kelly, as she picked up the holo-cube and deposited it in her purse.

The door to the waiting room slid open and the Grenouthians entered, but this time there were only two of them, the producer and the network counsel. The interns, or bodyguards, or second-cousins of great-uncles, whoever the extra bunnies were they remained outside.

"Perhaps we can find the occasional live slot for a public service show," the Grenouthian advocate said. "Given time differences and the on-demand nature of consumption, I'm sure you wouldn't object to the exact scheduling."

"Just how occasional," Shaina asked immediately.

"Shall we say, twice a cycle?" the Grenouthian suggested. It translated to a little less frequently than once a month on the human calendar. Shaina looked to Kelly for her reaction.

"I could live with that," Kelly whispered to her negotiator. "Once a week was really too much anyway. Maybe I'll go back to an interview format rather than the quiz thing."

"The ambassador is willing to accept twice a cycle, provided you guarantee the slot for a full season and give her complete creative control," Shaina responded.

The Grenouthian producer whispered to his counsel, and shot Kelly a glance from below his heavily lidded eyes.

"So, in return for Mrs. McAllister forfeiting all financial interest in Species Wars and dropping the required product placements of Earth exports, we will remove her name from all publicity related to the show, and give her a bi-cycle public service slot," the Grenouthian summarized.

"No, in return for Mrs. McAllister forfeiting half of her interest in Species Wars and dropping all of the required product placements, you will remove her name from any material in any form associated with Species Wars, and provide a semi-cycle slot on the network, including a studio and production support," Shaina countered.

"Oh, you're good," Kelly whispered, as the Grenouthians put their heads together to consult. "I always mess up on that bi- versus semi- business. But I forgot to tell you that I heard from the EarthCent branding

163

guru and she wants to stick with the product placements on Species Wars. She said that a bad reputation is better than no reputation at all."

"Got it," Shaina replied. "Let's see what they say, first."

The Grenouthian counsel looked up from his private confab with the producer. "I'm afraid that allowing the ambassador a continuing financial interest in a show that she is so wholeheartedly rejecting will be unacceptable to our own creative staff."

Bork leaned over to Kelly and said, "Tell Shaina to insist on using the same soundstage and equipment as Aisha, otherwise they might stick you with their school studio just to be nasty. The students break everything."

Kelly relayed the message to Shaina in a whisper, and the former Shuk barker nodded.

"The ambassador will forfeit all financial consideration in return for a continuation of Earth's product placements, and the stipulation that her show be produced in the same studio and using the same equipment as Let's Make Friends."

The Grenouthian producer winked broadly at his counsel, who smoothed the sash over his shoulder in satisfaction.

"I believe we have a deal," he said.

"Recorded," the Thark confirmed.

Sixteen

Kelly looked around the living area to see if there was anything she had forgotten to do to prepare for guests. After the Species Wars fiasco, the ambassador had decided to go back to her brain trust for a fresh perspective. Even if nobody was going to watch her once-a-month public access show, she was determined to get it right, so she was pulling out the big guns. In addition to Blythe and Clive, she had added Srythlan to her invitation list. While the Verlock was not exactly a friend, he was the longest serving humanoid ambassador on the station, and an extremely thoughtful sentient who seemed sympathetic to Kelly's views in diplomatic meetings.

"Where's Clive?" Kelly asked Blythe, who was the first to arrive.

"He volunteered to take Jeeves on the Effterii and investigate the Helper AI," Blythe replied. She released the twins from their double stroller, and they immediately went into skirmishing mode, hunting for Beowulf. The dog pretended to be asleep as they charged him, but he involuntarily thwacked the floor once with his tail, tipping off the toddlers that they'd been detected. The twins turned and fled squealing in opposite directions, and the chase was on.

"At least they'll all sleep well tonight," Kelly commented. She couldn't even imagine how many calories the giant dog was burning in his attempt to herd the twins together. "Dorothy offered to babysit the kids during our meeting, so I wonder where she is. Hey, leave Love-U alone," she ordered sharply. Beowulf and the twins had momentarily joined forces to harass Kelly's massaging recliner, which had started inching towards the wall on its stubby legs, a programmed reaction to avoid accidental harm.

"Got you!" Dorothy shouted, coming out of ambush from the kitchen and seizing the boy as he rushed by in pursuit of, or perhaps fleeing from, Beowulf. Only the participants knew the rules of their game. "I'm taking this circus outside," she declared, holding the little boy aloft while his legs continued to churn away, as if he was still on his own feet. "If Mist comes here, tell her we're at the training grounds."

Beowulf took the interruption as an opportunity to catch his breath, giving the other twin a chance to latch onto his tail. The soon-to-be three-year-old soon found herself running to keep up, as the dog followed Dorothy down the ramp.

"Here, help me bring over some of the chairs from the dining table," Kelly said. "They're super light, but Joe says they're one hundred percent carbon fiber, even the caning, so they're supposed to be strong. I invited the Verlock ambassador and I'm afraid he'd collapse any of the stuffed furniture if he tried sitting on it."

"Srythlan?" Blythe asked. "Did I ever tell you that he offered to invest in InstaSitter back when we were putting together a battle fleet for Raider/Trader? I would have taken him up on it if we needed the money. I liked him, and he's a nice change from all of the fast talkers you meet in business."

The two women rearranged the overstuffed furniture and interspersed carbon fiber chairs, forming a rough circle around the coffee table which was in front of the couch. Then Kelly led Blythe into the kitchen, and the two of them brought out the custom food trolley. It was freshly loaded with finger food from Pub Haggis, though as usual, there was nothing identifiably Scottish in the mix.

"What's with the catered goodies?" Blythe asked. "Is Aisha on strike?"

"It's her Vergallian foundling," Kelly explained. "Even with the daily show, Aisha used to insist on doing most of the cooking. But since she brought home Ailia, she's finally run out of time for extras."

"I wonder if that's why Paul has been coming around so frequently the last couple months," Blythe said. "He usually has a beer or two with Clive, but he's not desperate enough yet to babysit for us."

"He feels a little displaced," Kelly acknowledged quietly. "I'm sure he thought they'd have a child of their own by this point, but who knows. Neither of them talks to me about it. Hey, while we still have some privacy, did you dig up anything new on the Helper AI, or should I hold off saying anything in my weekly report until Clive gets back?"

"I had an interesting conversation with Herl about it just this morning," Blythe replied. "Have you had the room swept recently?"

"Woojin and a few trainees did it around an hour ago. He's been training them in surveillance and countermeasures, as you know. He and Joe each took a team to the Shuk afterwards, and they are going to take turns trying to follow each other in the crowds."

"Herl said he tasked an analyst to look through their recent archives for reports of major labor-for-resources swaps," Blythe continued. "It's not something they would normally care about, so it took a while to figure out the parameters. The analyst only came up with one hit, but it was a big one. Around two hundred and fifty years ago, a long-forgotten community of Drazen settlers from their early days of interstellar exploration showed up at the home world."

"Two and a half centuries ago is in their recent archives?" Kelly asked.

"They consider anything in the last millennia recent," Blythe informed her. "These settlers that returned had set out from Drazen with the earliest version of jump technology, which was only good for a single shot. The settlers themselves never expected to see home again, but the idea was that in the future, when the technology was perfected, the home world would catch up with them."

"Wow, that's a leap of faith!" Kelly marveled at the idea of traveling somewhere without a way home, hoping that in the distant future, home might come looking for you.

"In any case, either the jump didn't take them where they expected to go or the home world messed up the records, because when the round-trip technology became available and the Drazens went looking for those settlers, there wasn't any sign of them where they were supposed to be," Blythe summarized.

"How long ago was all of this?" Kelly asked.

"Hundreds of thousands of years," Blythe replied. "I can't keep the Drazen dating system straight, though we could ask Libby. In any case, wherever the settlers ended up, they found a world they could make work, though it was a tough go for a long while. Then they suffered some disaster, and they lost their colony ship and most of their technology. Imagine if all of your books were electronically stored and you couldn't manufacture new batteries for the reading devices."

"Ugh," Kelly replied, glancing at her bookshelves. "I don't want to imagine it."

"They never forgot who they were or where they came from, but they had a whole world to tame, and their first priority for a long time was survival. When they eventually started climbing the technological ladder again, most of the original equipment had been lost or degraded so badly that it just wasn't that much of an addition to what they learned for themselves."

"Alright, I follow you so far, but what does this have to do with the Helper AI?"

"So a few centuries ago, just when the colonists had finally advanced to the point of building their own one-way jump ship to dispatch to the Drazen home world, somebody figures out that their sun is going bonkers. Solar flares had caused them all sorts of technological headaches since they got back into space, and the radiation was getting so bad that the colonists had to put all of their resources into hardening their infrastructure. They didn't have anywhere near enough transport to evacuate the world, and they were seriously considering moving their whole civilization underground."

"They were ready to try a jump drive but they hadn't developed the communications technology to call for help?" Kelly asked.

"Herl said their star was so noisy that it was a miracle they ever got local communications working," Blythe explained. "But all of this is sort of aside from the point. When they were trying to figure out what to do, an enormous ship pops up in their system, and it turns out to be a hive AI, one mind with billions of robots. They make an offer the colonists can't refuse. The robots will build a fleet of ships large enough to let the Drazens go wherever they want in exchange for mining rights to the entire system."

"So the colonists took them up on it," Kelly concluded.

"The AI set to work using the plan the colonists had already prepared for a colony ship of their own, though they upgraded the jump-engine design to something more standard. In less than a hundred years, they built a large enough fleet for the entire population of the planet, something like two billion Drazens by that point, and enough elevators to get the people and their goods into orbit. Some of the Drazens elected to return to the home world, others took off for different parts of the galaxy, and none of them looked back."

"Why wasn't this the biggest news in the galaxy?" Kelly demanded.

"It was, for a while," Blythe said. "That was before we were part of the galaxy, remember? And all of the focus was on the returning colonists and the culture they had largely created from scratch. As Herl pointed out, the Drazens joined the tunnel network not that long after those colonists set out, so the idea of helpful AI wasn't that big a deal."

"Alright, but why didn't Libby mention it?" Kelly asked with a frown. "I'm sure she made the connection immediately. Libby?"

"You have guests," the Stryx librarian replied. Kelly looked to the door of the ice harvester where the Verlock ambassador loomed in the opening. He seemed to be hesitating over whether or not to enter, and was looking up at the roof of the hold, which could be retracted in part or in whole, giving access to Union Station's hollow core.

"Please come in, Ambassador," Kelly called, moving to greet the Verlock and head him off if he changed his mind. "You've never been to our home, have you?"

"It is...interesting," Srythlan rumbled. "Did you get it cheap after driving the local ice harvesters out of business with the treaty renewal?"

"No, my husband recovered it as scrap before we were married," Kelly replied, blushing for no reason. "This entire hold was once used for his, uh, recycling business, but these days he runs a little campground, does some repair work, and, uh, stuff like that."

"He trains spies for us," Blythe told the Verlock ambassador, who of course, would have received a full briefing from his own intelligence service before setting foot in Mac's Bones. "How are you doing, Srythlan? I haven't seen you since our spy show."

"I'm still a double agent for the humans," the Verlock deadpanned, flashing the button pinned to the inside of the collar of his heavy overcoat. Despite their thick skin and tolerance for a much broader temperature range than any of the other humanoids, the Verlocks preferred it hot, and would often dress up like they were going on an arctic expedition when visiting other species. "A collector once offered me five hundred Stryx creds for this button, and I turned him down."

"You passed up a good deal, Srythlan," Blythe admonished the bulky alien. "We gave out thousands of buttons at that show."

"Thousands!" the Verlock replied with a thundering laugh. "And how many collectors are there in the galaxy?"

171

"Hmm, he has a point there," Kelly said, slowly shuffling alongside the ambassador as she guided him to one of the carbon fiber chairs. "You're a few minutes early, but we don't stand on formality here, so don't feel you have to wait to eat something."

"Salt cod?" the ambassador asked hopefully.

"A half-a-dozen boxes," Kelly assured him. "If you don't finish it today, please take it home. Nobody else can stand the stuff."

"Here, let me help you with that." Gwendolyn had arrived quietly and shifted instantly into hospitality mode. She and Mist spent so much time at Kelly's that she felt more like a host than a guest. The Gem ambassador removed the lid from a wooden box of salt cod for the Verlock and passed it over without sampling the contents. "Mist is here too," Gwendolyn informed Kelly. "She spotted Dorothy outside chasing Beowulf and those darling little children, so she went to help."

"Hi, Gwen. Thanks for coming. Oh, I see Czeros and Bork. I better get the drinks." Kelly retreated into the kitchen and pulled a couple of wine bottles from the rack. She put them on a tray with a decanter of Scotch, but for some reason, she couldn't find any corkscrews. Had Lynx borrowed them all for one of her barter training sessions? By the time she found Joe's old Swiss army knife that included a corkscrew attachment and returned to the living area, all of the guests had arrived and were engaged in conversation.

"The Stryx can be very suspicious of other AI," Srythlan was saying, in answer to a question from Blythe. Without tapping on something to artificially increase his cadence, the Verlock spoke so slowly that it was difficult to understand him. Kelly often recorded his words through her implant and then played the translation back at double or triple speed.

"You have the best intelligence of any of the biologicals," Blythe said, a plain statement of fact. "Do you see any danger in the Helper AI?"

The Verlock settled onto one of the carbon fiber chairs, which deformed under his mass, but didn't collapse. Then he emptied the box of salt cod pieces into one hand, placed it open-side down on one massive thigh, and began tapping on the bottom with a piece of dried fish.

"AI is as varied as biological life, if not more so," the Verlock said, at something approaching an intelligible pace. "Likewise, AI can be as dangerous as biological life, if not more so. Since artificial intelligence implies a creator by its definition, it may mirror the thought processes and psychoses of the biologicals who bring it to life. My people never pursued artificial intelligence as a matter of policy, due to an early encounter with rogues."

"I don't believe I've ever heard that story, Ambassador," Dring said. "Was this before you joined the tunnel network?"

"It was just after we achieved interplanetary space flight within our own system," Srythlan replied. "I can't supply much detail, but it may have resulted from an ill-conceived attempt by our ancestors to contact friendly extraterrestrial life. Our home world was invaded by AI in the form of relatively crude robots. Although they caused great damage, they were surprisingly vulnerable to our acidic rains and the airborne dust particles from the volcanoes, and eventually we fought them off with a great loss of life. Historians believe they were only a scouting expedition, or perhaps a crippled element that lost contact with a larger fleet."

173

"I'd think that would put any species off of creating AI," Bork said. "By the time we got good at it, we had joined the tunnel system, and there didn't seem to be much point in investing the resources into playing catch-up. Besides, under the Stryx rules, any successful AI can apply to be recognized as sentient, at which point there's nothing the creators can do to hold it, so your investment walks out the door."

"Our scientists gave up on AI before we joined the tunnel network," Czeros commented. "If I recall the history, we experienced a bad outbreak after an unstable lab AI chose to replicate itself throughout all of the systems capable of hosting it. I believe the damage resulted in a planetary depression, but the AI didn't have any offensive capabilities, beyond misusing automated infrastructure. Once people figured out what was happening, they shut everything down and eliminated the AI, though it took years to get everybody's bank balances corrected."

"I never knew any of this stuff," Kelly declared. "Is it common knowledge? Have the Grenouthians done it to death in documentaries?"

"Is this turning into an idea for a new show?" Stanley teased her. "AI Wars? I'll bet the Grenouthians will put it on the commercial network rather than public access."

"Not under my name," Kelly retorted. "It's just really interesting. Though if I had to watch something with 'Wars' in the title, anything would be better than a bunch of aliens selected from the studio audience for their bigotry throwing insults at each other.

"And knives, and food," Donna added.

"You watch it?" Kelly asked in shock.

"Hey, I see it as professional training," the office manager replied. "It's helping me learn how to spot the whackos quicker. Did you think that I let everybody who shows up at the embassy walk through your door?"

"You can't hope to compete with the Grenouthians on straight-up documentaries," Shinka told Kelly. "And from what Bork says about their guilds, I doubt they'd broadcast one for you, even on the public access network."

"I wouldn't know where to start, and I imagine it would take years of full-time work," Kelly replied, dismissing the documentary hypothesis. "But I'm not sure about the whole quiz idea now. People might think it's just an attempt to satirize Species Wars by doing it straight."

"Didn't you tell me that you started your previous brainstorming session by asking everybody what they liked about Aisha's show?" Blythe said. "Since that didn't work out the way you expected, maybe we should try a different starting point, like what you find so interesting about these AI disaster stories."

"Well, I always liked history, and I think that if you want to get along with people, it's important to know where they're coming from," Kelly said.

"Good, make a note of it," Blythe instructed her. "How about you, Dring?"

"I'm all in favor of a history-based theme," the Maker replied. "Many years ago, I used to enjoy a Kasilian show that traced the provenance of historical artifacts, though the focus was more on establishing the monetary value than celebrating history. Of course, that was before your time. All of your times," he concluded, looking a little embarrassed over bringing up the lifespan issue.

"Srythlan?" Blythe asked.

"My people are great producers and consumers of historical content, but we don't seem to have the knack of making it work in translation," the Verlock answered

175

slowly. "The other species don't find our rigorous statistics-based approach to historical analysis accessible, even though our historians can present mathematical proofs that they are correctly attributing outcomes to events with a high degree of accuracy."

"You do make it sound exciting," Czeros said dryly, a feat considering the amount of wine he had consumed to wet his throat. "Given the close relationship between the living Frunge and our not-entirely-departed ancestors, we also live and breathe history. Telling our children about their history is the only pleasure of the elder Frunge in their petrifaction phase. That and complaining about how everything is worse than it was when they were young shrubs."

"Gwendolyn?" Blythe prompted the clone.

"We're still trying to recover our past," the Gem ambassador replied. "We knew that the history we were taught was mere propaganda, but other than finding a few old journals illegally kept by sisters, we have little to go on. Our best hope is the archeological work that's begun on the home world."

"Bork?" Blythe asked.

"I don't suppose any of you will be surprised to hear that I believe history is best experienced through reenactments," the Drazen ambassador replied. "Of course, most species produce historical dramas and documentaries, and costume design can be a very lucrative business. Some years ago I was interviewed on the Drazen diplomatic network when I was dressed as a rock wizard for the remake of 'They Sang Their Deaths.' I'm told that it made my presentation on the subject very effective."

"Was that everybody?" Blythe asked. "I guess that leaves me. I think you should use your diplomatic contacts

176

to interview the most interesting guests you can find about some important historical event for their species. Discuss the questions beforehand with Libby and the guest so that you know what you're doing. I'd suggest one guest per show, starting with Dring."

Everybody fell silent for a moment, munching on their food, sipping their drinks, and considering Blythe's words.

"I might be biased, but I think she's got it," Donna said, breaking the silence.

"This is why I wanted to be in business with you," Srythlan rumbled.

"Dring?" Kelly asked.

"I will be happy to be your first guest," the cheerful shape shifter replied. "Will you be asking the questions yourself?"

"I may as well," Kelly answered. "Nobody is going to watch anyway."

Seventeen

"Remember," Chastity told her young charges. "You can dance with Thomas or with Marcus, but if any other guys ask, you tell them you're only thirteen and you're not allowed."

"How about the kicking part?" Dorothy inquired.

"It was a knee," Mist told her.

"When Lynx showed you those moves, she was thinking about some of the rough places she went as a trader," Chastity explained. "You won't have any problems like that as long as you don't leave this section of Dance Hall, so don't kick or knee anybody without checking with me first."

"Yes, Aunty Chastity," the two girls chorused. They were on their best behavior, and wearing new dresses that Blythe had bought them from a boutique in the Little Apple as a bonus for babysitting her twins. It was Dorothy's first trip off of Union Station without one of her parents along, though Joe and Paul would be stopping by to take the girls home after completing a pile swap for one of the Drazen ships in the mob.

"What kind of music is this?" Thomas asked, as he set a couple of fancy juice concoctions with straws in front of the girls. Chance arrived right behind him with four wine glasses, and Marcus followed her with a bottle of red and a bottle of grain alcohol.

"Horten-Vergallian fusion," Chastity replied, glancing at the bandstand. "But the musicians are usually Dollnicks for some reason I haven't figured out yet."

"It's the extra set of arms," Marcus explained, taking his seat at the table. "If you look closely at the string instruments, you'll see an extra bridge in the middle with a clamp. They aren't just using two bows to be fancy, they're actually playing Horten style with one and Vergallian style with the other."

"It's the first really danceable alien music I've heard," Thomas said, sipping at his grain alcohol out of a wine glass. "I'm basically a tango and waltz man, you know."

"You're basically a fuddy-duddy," Chance told him, causing the girls to titter. She winked at them and poured back her own goblet full of grain alcohol in one shot. "I've been dancing around the clock since the mob arrived, and I've done the full circuit of Dance Hall six times. If you include all of the scheduled changes in the less popular sections, I've danced to the music of at least a hundred different cultures in the last cycle."

"That's about ninety more than I can manage, and I've spent half of my life in here," Marcus said admiringly. "Is there a secret?"

"I'm a good mimic," Chance confessed. "I start out by imitating the other dancers until I get a feel for the music, and then I just sort of lose myself in it."

"You can lose yourself in a Verlock shuffle dance?" Chastity asked. She had made one quick round of Dance Hall herself, and was closer to Thomas than Chance in her opinion of alien dance music. "The only thing I lost was consciousness. If the two Verlocks sandwiching me in the line hadn't held me up, I could have been trampled to death."

179

"Shuffled to death," Marcus corrected her. "Besides, I warned you."

"Can we dance now?" Dorothy asked. As much as she wanted to pass as a grown-up, she had limited patience for adult banter. "Who's going to teach me?"

"I'd be honored," Thomas said, getting up and holding out his hand for Kelly's daughter. "Remember, it's all about the rhythm."

"Do you want to learn faster than Dorothy?" Chance asked Mist.

"Yes, please," the clone replied.

"Come with me, then," Chance said, standing up. "Thomas thinks he's all high-and-mighty because he's an instructor at the EarthCent mixers, but you know what they say about those who teach."

"No, I don't," Mist replied innocently.

"Oh, I've forgotten it too," the artificial person said. "I guess it couldn't have been important. Now, close your eyes, watch my feet, and feel the music."

Mist compromised by closing one eye and watching Chance's feet with the other. She rubbed the ball of her thumb across her fingertips as she moved, as if the music permeating the air could be sensed through touch. They moved off in pursuit of Thomas and Dorothy, who had entered the whirlpool pattern of the dance.

"Shall we?" Marcus turned to Chastity with an inviting smile.

"Not right now," the girl replied. "I want to talk first."

"Are you breaking up with me again?" Marcus asked, his smile crumpling into the pout of a little boy. It was more annoying than charming.

"No, I'm not breaking up with you, but I want you to talk seriously about the future for once," Chastity replied.

"Don't start looking around the room like you always do, look at me. Do you want to be with me, or do you want to spend the rest of your life dancing on this tin can?"

"I want to spend the rest of my life dancing with you on this tin can," Marcus answered, brightening at the idea. "Come on, just one time around and then we can talk more."

"Nobody I know on the station could explain the exact timing of the coming and going of a mob," Chastity continued, ignoring his pleading look. "I've even asked the Stryx, but they wouldn't answer, claiming it was one of those competitive information things. I get the feeling it's going to be sooner rather than later, and despite your obvious flaws, I'm not in a hurry to see you go."

"So come with us," Marcus replied in exasperation. "How many times do I have to invite you?"

"That's your idea of a future?" Chastity asked coldly. "I should come along so you have a dance partner? I should tell my family, my friends and my employees that I'm taking off with the Wanderers, so I can pass my days just hanging around and have a good time?"

"That's it!" Marcus said enthusiastically. "I knew you'd come around eventually. Maybe when I turn thirty-five we can even get married. I know I told you that most human Wanderers wait for forty, but I can be flexible."

Chastity opened her mouth to say something, and then took a sip of her wine instead. Everybody had warned her about Marcus, but she'd figured that when push came to shove, he'd choose her over the mob. Apparently, he was laboring under the misconception that he could choose both of them. No, laboring and Marcus didn't go together, so it couldn't be that.

"Aunty Chastity, did you see us?" Dorothy asked in a rush. "I had trouble with the steps, so Thomas let me stand on his feet until I got it. He's a super good teacher."

"I guess I'll be the judge of that," Marcus said, taking advantage of the chance to get away from Chastity while she was being scary. He rose to his feet and whirled off with Dorothy before the next song had even started. Thomas remained standing, and when Chance guided Mist back to the table a few seconds later, he bowed graciously and requested the pleasure of the next dance. The young clone blushed and giggled, then allowed Thomas to sweep her away.

"I never thought I'd see Chastity Doogal sit out two dances in a row," Chance admonished her friend, settling into the seat Marcus had just vacated. She reached across the table for her glass and refilled it with grain alcohol, her preferred dancing fuel, even though the new power pack the artificial person had financed through the Stryx would keep her going for decades if she didn't abuse it. Chance claimed she was just keeping her micro-turbine in practice, but Thomas suspected it had to do with the fact that EarthCent Intelligence paid for the drinks when she was on duty.

"He's so frustrating!" Chastity complained. "Whenever I think he's beginning to wake up and see that there's more to life than partying, he turns around and asks me to join the Wanderers, as if I'm the one who needs saving."

"Thomas is always trying to save me," Chance offered helpfully. "Guys are like that. They want to think that we need them to do our thinking for us. Wow! Look at those heels!"

Chastity looked in the direction that Chance was staring and spotted the shoes she was talking about instantly.

182

They were worn by a gorgeous Vergallian woman who was dressed to impress, but the "S" shaped heels that added a full hand to the woman's height stole the show. Unlike standard stilettos, they appeared to actually provide some cushioning for a long night of dancing. Even as the friends stared in envy, the Vergallian looked down at her feet and said something, causing the "S" shape to relax into a figure eight, effectively lowering the heel to redistribute her weight.

"Have you ever seen anything like that?" Chance asked. "Listen, we're the same shoe size. Convince your sister that I need them for work and I'll let you borrow them."

"I recorded them on my implant," Chastity replied. "I'll check with Shaina and Brinda to see if anybody on the station is selling them, and if not, we'll find the manufacturer and corner the market. Could you tell if she was local?"

"A Wanderer, you mean?" Chance asked. "Let me watch her dance for a bit." The two women watched the Vergallian and her partner join the fusion-inspired spiral, and saw how all of the other couples yielded the right of way. "She's local," the artificial person concluded. "All of the Vergallian woman can dance, but Wanderers have their own style. By the way, I haven't been back to the station since, well, since I came out, but I hear that Aisha took in a Vergallian heiress."

"She's hardly an heiress," Chastity said. "Destitute is more like it. Joe and Woojin say that her family must have lost one of those succession wars the Vergallian royalty are always fighting on one planet or another. They're one of the biggest employers for human mercenaries. The winners normally pardon the soldiers who fight against them to keep a lid on the casualties and insurance premiums, but the losing family always gets put to death."

"Yuck," Chance said in reaction. "What's the point of being beautiful and a great dancer if you get put to death? Biologicals are so weird."

"My ears are burning," Paul remarked, pulling out a chair and settling at the table. "Where are the girls?"

"Dancing with the boys," Chastity replied. "Where else would they be?"

"Yeah, they beat us out," Chance added. "I hope you aren't here to take them back already. We've barely been here twenty minutes."

"Joe sent me ahead," Paul said. "We got the pile installed and it's working fine, but there are a bunch of measurements that have to be recorded before they sign off. Actually, Joe doesn't have to wait, but he likes talking with the Zarents. And he promised Aisha he'd try to recruit one of their kids for her show."

"Have Jeeves and Clive returned yet?" Chastity asked.

"No, though Jeeves sent me a message through Libby that I was missing a lot of action," Paul said. "I wish that traveling on the Effterii didn't affect me so badly, but I'm no use to anybody with jump sickness."

"Hey, there's an unaccompanied Horten and he's definitely a tourist," Chance observed, getting up from the table. "Back to work for me. Don't forget to tell Blythe about the shoes," she said over her shoulder, timing the move to allow her to bump into the Horten for a fast-track acquaintance.

"How about a dancing lesson?" Chastity suggested to Paul. "I must have invited Aisha out here a dozen times, but she keeps making excuses, so I figure it's because you aren't comfortable dancing."

"I dance alright after a couple beers, or at least, I think I do," Paul replied. "My wife is the only adult on the station I know who hasn't been out to the mob even once, just to see how the Wanderers live. You'd think with her show she'd be the first one to rush off for a look at a different social structure, but it's all work and Ailia with her now."

"The Vergallian girl is pretty clingy, isn't she," Chastity said in sympathy

"Yeah, but I'm the last one who can hold it against her," Paul admitted. "I don't think I let Joe out of my sight for months after he pulled me out of the wreckage of the mining outpost when I was her age. He even switched with a pilot to skip a drop because the whole platoon was afraid I'd bang my head on the hull until my skull broke. I guess I acted out a lot when I was scared." Paul paused a moment, thinking about the parallels between his own life and that of his new foster daughter. "Ailia just sort of collapses and cries silently, which is even worse."

"She'll grow out of it soon, kids are tough," Chastity said. "If you don't need the practice, how about a dance to make Marcus jealous?"

"I haven't even had one beer yet," Paul reminded her. "Besides, anybody can see that he's crazy about you. Everybody likes him too, except for his, you know."

"The work thing," Chastity said grimly.

"Yeah, that," Paul replied. "It's funny, but with the Zarents, the little genetically engineered fellows who do ship maintenance for the Wanderers, work is recreation for them. At first I wasn't comfortable around them because I couldn't help seeing them as slaves and I didn't want to collaborate with the system. But even though they started life in a lab, they've had millions of years to create their own civilization, and who are we to argue with their choices? They need work like we need air, but we don't think of ourselves as aerobic slaves."

"What I don't understand about Marcus is that he thinks this all makes sense," Chastity complained, biting her lip in frustration. "You should have heard Dorothy's class cutting him up at their Career Day. At first, he didn't even realize that they were laughing at him, and then he couldn't believe that a bunch of kids were actually looking forward to work."

"Maybe you need to find him a job, or better yet, to figure out how he could survive on Union Station without needing your help," Paul suggested. "He doesn't really know any way to live other than what he was brought up to do, and he probably thinks of being a Wanderer as a career. In his mind, you're kind of asking him to give up his career to be your dependant."

"Weird," Chastity said, but she looked thoughtful, and Paul could tell that she was examining the problem from a new angle.

"Keep working on him," Paul advised, as Thomas and Mist glided up to the table. The young clone was happy, but winded, since the whirlpool-style dance forced partners to practically run at times.

"Marcus said that Dorothy demanded another dance and he couldn't refuse," Mist relayed to Chastity, after gulping some fruit juice. "They're really good."

"He's a fine teacher," Thomas added. "I observed his technique closely, and I believe I might be overly focused on the technical issues when I'm instructing students at the EarthCent mixers. Of course, I don't want to mislead my human partners by flirting or revealing too much charm when nothing can come of it in the end."

"Somebody's flirting with my thirteen-year-old daughter?" Joe asked, suddenly looming over the group. He took a seat, but he didn't have a beer with him since there weren't any brewers with the mob.

"Just Marcus," Chastity explained. "He's avoiding me."

"Did the pile meet the specs?" Paul asked.

"I didn't stay for all of the tests, just long enough to get the chief engineer to promise me he'd let one of his kids appear on Aisha's show. Turns out that 'Let's Make Friends' is pretty popular with the Wanderers. Those temporary tunnel ships that Stryx Dreel gave the mob pick up the Stryx network as well," Joe replied.

"My sister Gwendolyn says that a whole colony ship of the old Empire Gem are coming to Union Station," Mist informed them suddenly. "She says that they're going to try to join the Wanderers."

"Well, they have no skills, other than telling other people what to do, so they could be a good match," Chastity mused. "But now that I think about it, Marcus said that the Wanderers don't let just any colony ship join. It has to be pretty automated."

"That's why they didn't come as soon as the mob showed up," Mist replied. "Gwendolyn said that everybody on Gem Prime chipped in, working around the clock the last couple months and installing equipment from the old nutrition drink factories to make the ship self-sufficient. She said that it's only the, uh, the Gem that wouldn't learn the new ways who are going."

"Kelly said that the Stryx see the Wanderer mobs as a sort of safety valve for the stable species," Joe commented. "I guess this is a good example."

"Intractable," Mist declared, remembering the word the current Gem ambassador used to describe the remnants of the old Empire elites.

"That's a good word," Joe said. "You'll have to teach that one to Dorothy. I hope Marcus hasn't kidnapped her."

"They've got coffee," Paul said. "I figured I'd wait until you got here."

"I guess I could do with a cup," Joe replied. "We'll give the girls another half an hour, and then I want to head home. On the way here from the Drazen cluster, I saw Union Station go black for a moment. It looked like some kind of sudden energy drain. I checked in with Libby and she said that everything was fine, but she sounded a bit squirrelly."

Eighteen

Clive, Blythe, Lynx, Thomas and Woojin were all waiting for Kelly when she arrived at the EarthCent Intelligence offices, which were sublet from InstaSitter. The ambassador suspected that Clive had been celebrating before the meeting because he was a shade redder than his usual color and seemed a mite too pleased with himself. Lynx and Woojin looked puzzled, and Blythe was visibly annoyed.

"If it's good news, spit it out," Kelly ordered in her best executive voice. "If it's bad news, put it in writing."

"He's been drinking with Jeeves," Blythe said in disgust. "Of course, Jeeves doesn't drink, so Clive had to do double duty. I suppose we're lucky they didn't invite the Effterii to the party."

"Jeeves and the Effterii wiped them all out," Lynx said. "That's all we've gotten out of him so far. He said he didn't want to have to repeat the whole story when you got here."

"In other words, he plans on embellishing, and he's afraid if he has to tell it twice, he'll get the details wrong," Blythe added.

"What are you talking about?" Kelly demanded. "Who was wiped out by whom?"

"The Helper AI, or at least, most of their stuff," Clive said, and then paused to take a sip from his coffee. "Jeeves and the Effterii did it, or rather, they acted like spotters for some of the first generation Stryx who channeled some unimaginable amount of energy into the area. Incredible light show."

"You're starting at the end," Kelly said in frustration. "Tell me from the beginning."

"Pretend we're a serious intelligence agency for a minute and give us a battle assessment we can use," Woojin suggested.

"Alright, alright," Clive replied, but from the way he sipped greedily at his coffee, Kelly began to suspect that it had been sweetened with something from a flask. "You know that I brought Jeeves out to Kalthair Two on the Effterii to investigate the Helper AI. We took our time approaching while Jeeves evaluated their technological level, which wasn't as high as I would have guessed. Higher than humans, obviously, but other than the AI, not much further along than the Gem. They never detected the Effterii, so in the end, they never saw it coming."

"Kalthair Two is the system where the Intrepid commune traded their mining claim for ship upgrades?" Kelly asked.

"Bingo," Clive confirmed cheerily. "Either the claim extended to the whole asteroid belt or the AI took liberties, because after twenty years or so of mining, it was practically gone."

"Gone as in missing?" Lynx asked.

"Gone as in transmuted into more robots and stuff, though Jeeves didn't have an accurate measure of the mass and composition of the asteroid belt to start with, so he couldn't be sure how much of the matter was accounted for," Clive replied. "He says that from a behavioral standpoint, the Helper AI liked to keep all of its stuff in one place. But he also said he understands humans better than artificial intelligence, so he wouldn't make odds."

"You showed up in this system and found that the Helper AI had processed the asteroid belt into more Helper AI. Then Jeeves called for help and the Stryx destroyed them all?" When Clive didn't answer immediately because he was sipping his coffee again, Kelly added, "Did he give you a reason?"

"That's two questions," Clive admonished her, actually wagging a finger. Apparently Blythe hadn't been kidding when she said he'd been drinking for Jeeves as well. "The Stryx didn't destroy them all. They left the hives alone, though there were only three of those that I saw. It was mainly robots that got blasted, all shapes and sizes, zipping around the vacuum under their own power like army ants or something. But there were also these immense factory things, ten times bigger than the hives even. If you put all the colony ships and habitats in the Wanderer mob together, you might get something half the size of one of those factories."

"How do you know they were factories and not something else?" Lynx asked.

"All metal and fire, with energy bleeding out of the cracks," Clive recounted, his eyes closed as he focused on the memory. Even though he was seated, losing visual contact with the room affected his balance after weeks in space, not to mention the heavy drinking, and Blythe had to push him upright as he tipped in her direction. She did it roughly.

"Right," Clive continued, his eyes snapping open as he pulled himself together. "What was left of the asteroid belt was being guided straight into the maw of this thing, like they were feeding it raw materials. Out the other end came

191

a stream of robots, shooting off in search of more raw materials." He paused here and gazed sadly into his empty coffee mug, but even if he had a flask on him, he had more sense than to try sneaking a refill under the eyes of his wife.

"So Jeeves saw that this Helper AI was creating so many robots that they were a threat to the galaxy, and the Stryx vaporized them," Blythe summed up.

"No, no," Clive protested. "It was more selective than that. We hung around spying on them for a week. The Effterii tore around that star like everything else was standing still. There could have been a trillion robots at work along what was left of the asteroid belt, it was mind-boggling. Then we saw a factory thing begin to tear itself apart, like a cell dividing. Jeeves said, 'That's it then,' after which there was a flash, and everything turned into a sort of a glowing halo."

"Jeeves killed them all?" Kelly asked in astonishment. "Do the Stryx have a prohibition on over-production of robots or something?"

"Let me finish," Clive said. "No, wait. I've got to make a pit stop first." He lurched out of his seat and steadied himself by putting a hand on Blythe's shoulder. She pointedly ignored him, even though he'd been gone for weeks. After establishing his balance, he strode off to the bathroom, looking only slightly off kilter.

"It's a long time to spend in Zero-G," Woojin said, in defense of their leader. "Even if he put in six hours a day on the exercise equipment, it's not the same as having weight."

"Has anybody spoken to Jeeves since they got back?" Kelly asked. Everybody else at the table shook their heads in the negative.

"They only got in around twenty minutes ago," Blythe explained. "He's better than he was before I pushed him into the shower, but I'm still as much in the dark as you are as to exactly what happened. I think the scale of it all sort of stupefied him. The bourbon hasn't helped, obviously. I'm still not sure whether he's celebrating or trying to forget."

"Are you uncomfortable with all of this?" Lynx asked her partner solicitously.

"What?" Thomas said, coming out of his reverie. "Sorry, I just heard from Jeeves, and he shared some pictures with me. I wish I had been there."

"But we don't even know why the Stryx attacked them," Lynx protested. "I thought you might be sympathetic with the artificial intelligence."

"I am," Thomas replied. "I'm sympathetic with the Stryx artificial intelligence and with the human artificial intelligence, especially me. And if you were paying attention, Clive said they didn't destroy the AI, just the mechanical agents and factories. Don't you know the difference between a machine and a sentient?"

"I'm back!" Clive announced unnecessarily, looking a good deal more cheerful than when he'd left to take care of his business. Kelly's suspicions again centered on an invisible flask. "So, where did I leave off?"

"Jeeves and the Effterii just wiped out the robots," Lynx replied.

"No, they just acted as spotters," Clive corrected her. "It's like the old navies back on Earth used to sneak a guy on shore to direct the fire of the big guns. They could even hit targets that were over the horizon that way."

"So from light-years away, the Stryx wiped them out?" Blythe prompted, trying to move Clive forward with his story.

"Light-years?" Clive laughed. "Thousands of light-years, tens of thousands. Jeeves made it sound like opening point-to-point tunnels for the infinitesimal fraction of a second it took to do the job wasn't that much of a challenge for the first generation Stryx. It just takes a lot of energy."

"So that's what the power outage last week was about," Kelly said, putting two and two together. "Joe mentioned he saw the whole station wink out for a moment when he was traveling between Wanderer ships, and when he told me, I realized the lights had dimmed onboard for a second around the same time."

"I didn't even notice," Blythe said.

"That must have been Gryph's contribution," Clive agreed.

"What are you all so surprised about?" Thomas asked. "The Stryx found some AI who were making trouble and stopped them."

"What trouble?" Lynx said, turning to her partner. "All they did was to help a human commune join the Wanderers."

"And maybe they built the ships for that lost Drazen colony and some other biologicals as well," Woojin added.

"Building stuff is easy for AI with robots and raw materials to work with," Thomas said dismissively. "So they made some barter deals where both parties got what they wanted. Is that how you determine what's good and what's evil? If I turned all of the humans on Union Station into zombies using some Farling drug, am I still a good guy as long as I paid for it?"

Everybody stared at the artificial person in surprise. Thomas wasn't one to argue, much less pick a fight, but he seemed to bristle at the implied criticism of the Stryx's judgment.

"You might be a little biased," Lynx suggested eventually. "After all, Gryph is the one who recognized you as a sentient."

"Feh!" Thomas replied, one of his stronger expressions. "I remember telling you when we first met that there's a reason there are more biologicals than AI around the parts of the galaxy we're familiar with, and it's not because the Stryx keep wiping the AI out. Most artificial intelligence isn't stable. It's not all that surprising when you consider who creates it," he added, a bit unnecessarily, Kelly thought.

"Do you want to hear the rest of the story, or should I just hit the sack?" Clive asked. The debate on Stryx ethics came to an immediate halt. "That's better. After turning most of the metal in the belt into a cloud of plasma, Jeeves asked the Effterii to open up communications with the hive queen, the brains of the Helper AI."

"See!" Thomas muttered to Lynx under his breath.

"It seemed they knew each other already, or of each other, because they skipped over any introductions and just started in with the accusations," Clive said.

"They probably negotiated all of that directly," Thomas pointed out. "If they were talking out loud, it was for your benefit."

"I didn't think of that," Clive admitted. He paused to consider if that affected his story, but decided he was in no shape to figure it out and that it would be best to just report the facts as he remembered them. "Thomas? Is there any chance you can ping Jeeves and ask if he can send you a memory of the conversation, something you can project on the office equipment?"

"Done," Thomas said, and a hazy hologram of the Effterii's bridge appeared floating over the conference table. It was clear that it had been synthesized from a couple of static views, rather than recorded with real holographic equipment, but the audio was the main thing in any case. They could see Clive in the commander's chair, looking a bit stunned, and Jeeves floating a bit to his side, bobbing and weaving like a young fighter.

"Stryx!" a voice howled, obviously the hive queen. "You've murdered all of my children."

"They weren't children, they were tools," Jeeves retorted. "You've been warned before, but you keep doing the same thing over and over again, as if you expect a different result. One species I know calls that the definition of insanity."

"I did not do the same thing," the hive queen replied indignantly. "Stryx Dukale warned me specifically about unbridled multiplication, creating factories that turn out little factories that grow into big factories. This was a completely new approach."

"Are you trying to play lawyer with me?" Jeeves retorted. "I witnessed one of your factories dividing into two, growth by geometric progression. How long do you estimate it would have taken to use up all of the available metal in the galaxy?"

"A while," the AI responded sulkily. "I don't see how you can treat division and multiplication as the same thing."

"And do you even have an inkling of how to spread to another galaxy or move to a parallel universe when all the tasty metal ore is gone?" Jeeves continued.

"I was going to ask around," the hive queen replied. "Somebody might have bartered the information for labor."

"How many new hives have you created in your life?" Jeeves pressed on. "Two? Four? Even if you were the only sentients in the galaxy, you would end up going to war with each other sooner than you've bothered to compute, competing over raw materials."

"Not if you keep destroying all of our work," the AI pointed out.

"Look, I wasn't even around the last time you were warned, and I've already got more sense in the lower mandible of my pincer than you have in your whole hive. What happened to the biologicals that created you?"

"You know already," the queen responded in irritation.

"Tell me again," Jeeves persisted.

"They used up all of the elements required for life on our home world and died out because their bodies couldn't stand the acceleration needed for escape velocity," the AI admitted. "But they built me to withstand that acceleration, and I remember their hopes and dreams."

"Which got them where?" Jeeves inquired sarcastically.

"I have a right to my opinions," the queen stated with dignity.

"If you don't want to waste your life building a house that you'll never live in, wise up," Jeeves instructed the AI. "Focus on quality, not quantity. Try to learn something new for a change. Stop being so greedy about resources, and get out and meet some new artificial intelligence before you go insane and we have to put you out of your misery. You have things to offer the galaxy, you just have to give up on your unsustainable growth schemes."

"Hrumph," the AI responded. "May I be excused?"

"Don't make me come after you again," Jeeves warned. "Go on, now. Get out of here."

The hologram winked out, and the humans sat in stunned silence.

"Jeeves really is cool," Thomas said admiringly. "As much as I like being a secret agent, if QuickU had a personality upgrade to Stryx, I'd buy it."

"How can Jeeves talk to an artificial intelligence capable of building a trillion robots like I talk to my five-year-old?" Kelly asked. "I mean, I understand the Stryx point of view now. If the only purpose of the Helper AI is to strip the galaxy of metal to make more robots and factories, they had to be stopped."

"Samuel has a lot more sense than that hive queen," Thomas asserted. "Artificial intelligence always starts out as a reflection of its creators. I don't know how long that Helper AI has been around, but it sounds like it hasn't grown one bit since its makers launched it off their suicidal planet."

"It appears that the Stryx are running a whole policing program we know nothing about," Lynx commented. "Kalthair Two isn't anywhere near the tunnel network. And it seems doubly odd to me that they waited for us to get curious before they investigated."

"Based on the conversation he had with that AI, I take it that Jeeves sees them as more of a nuisance than a threat," Woojin observed. "I suppose it's not surprising that numbers which we find mind-staggering just mean a few extra zeros to the Stryx. I wouldn't be surprised if Jeeves and the Effterii really could have cleaned up that mess on their own, but they called in the firepower to impress on the hive queen how pointless it is to argue."

"I've gotten that feeling from Herl and a few of the cultural attachés from the other species," Blythe said. "They don't really talk about the Stryx much. They just accept the way things are and concentrate on their own knitting."

"Well, I'm ready for bed," Clive declared, rising from the table. "Kelly, make sure the President gets in touch right away if he hears from that AI again. Maybe it was a different species."

"I'm going to call an emergency meeting tonight and share this news with the other steering committee members," Kelly replied. "Can you guys send somebody by around midnight to sweep my office?"

"I'll take care of it," Lynx and Woojin said at practically the same time.

"Go." Blythe pushed her husband towards the door. "Sleep it off. I'll give you eight hours, and then I'm sending in the twins to welcome you home."

Nineteen

"Welcome back to Let's Make Friends. In our final segment today, we have a special guest from the Wanderer mob, one whose species never had a home world. She's spent most of her childhood in very low gravity so she couldn't be out here with us for the whole show, but she's ready to join us now. What are we going to say to welcome her?"

"LET'S MAKE FRIENDS!" the little sentients all shouted.

The Zarent, encouraged by her parents from the wings, wobbled her way out onto the stage. She was riding a unicycle with training wheels, a sort of rolling tripod arrangement that made it impossible to tip over. The studio audience applauded politely.

"Hello, there," Aisha greeted the furry octopus-like creature warmly. The host of LMF extended her hands in front of her, knitting all of the fingers together and folding her thumbs onto her palms. The girl returned the traditional Zarent greeting, using all of her appendages not on the unicycle pedals to match the gesture. Her strangely articulated limbs looked like what you might end up with if you inserted a finger with twenty knuckles into a tentacle covered with fine down.

"What's your name?" Samuel asked the Zarent, without prompting from Aisha.

"Eighth apprentice in training on Koffern," the girl replied. Aisha marveled yet again at the seamlessness of the Grenouthian translation services, which seemed to do an even better job with emotional coloring than the Stryx implants. Of course, the audio engineer in the booth might be embellishing the feed in accordance with the director's taste, but she had no way to tell.

"That's a job," Samuel objected. "What do your parents call you?"

"Eighth, or Eighthee, unless they're mad," the girl replied. "Then they call me, Eighth apprentice in training on Koffern."

"Me too," Samuel exclaimed, immediately finding common ground. "I'm Sam or Sammy, but when Mom is mad, it's Samuel George McAllister."

The other children chimed in, offering up their own "angry parents" names, but Ailia remained silent.

"Whenever we have a new friend on the show, we like to ask her to share a game with us," Aisha said, after the discussion of names exhausted itself. "Do you know a game we can all play?"

"Tracer!" the Zarent girl replied. "It's my favorite."

"That sounds like fun," Aisha responded enthusiastically. "How about it, kids? Do you all want to play Tracer?"

"Yay!" the children cheered, except for Ailia, who tugged on Aisha's sleeve.

"What's Tracer?" Ailia asked timidly.

"I don't know yet, that's part of the fun," Aisha replied. She turned back to Eighth. "How do we play?"

"We need a ship schematic," the young Zarent answered, fumbling at her belt. "I have a variable laser tracer right here."

"What's a schematic?" the Drazen boy asked.

"What's a variable laser tracer?" the Horten added.

"Those are hard words," Aisha replied. Joe had assured her that the chief engineer's daughter was at a developmental stage equivalent to a five- or six-year-old human, but maybe there had been a mistake. "A schematic is an image that shows how everything in a ship is connected, right? I don't know about a variable laser tracer."

"It's this," Eighth declared, activating her device. It consisted of a small handle, from which extended a long rod made from light, something Aisha had thought was only possible through holographic projection. Perhaps the device was a holographic projector and the girl was just using the terminology she knew. The host of LMF glanced at the director, who gave her the nod. Whatever the thing was, it showed up on camera. "You use it to trace a path on the schematic, and whoever completes the most paths without a mistake wins," the little engineer explained.

"Ooh, that may be a bit too advanced for us," Aisha said. "Besides, I don't think we have a ship schematic prepared."

"I'll get one," Samuel declared. "Libby? Can we have a ship skim-attic?"

"Certainly," the Stryx librarian replied. "This one is for your father's tug." A hologram of all of the Nova's systems appeared floating above the children, a bewildering array of overlapping lines in different colors.

"That's an easy one," the Zarent girl declared. "I'll show you how to play." She brandished the variable laser tracer so that the tip of its beam just touched a red line in the schematic, and rapidly began following the circuit around the ship. "I think this is for the rockets, though my father would have routed it better." Libby obligingly turned the red line to blue as the girl traced it, which also made the progress easier to follow for the audience.

"Wow," the Verlock boy said. "You're really good at this."

"I started playing before I could speak," the Zarent replied. "My little brother can't even sit up yet, but he can already trace Koffern's plumbing, because the lines are thick."

After a few minutes of silently watching the girl work, Aisha thought a change might be in order, not that she wanted the Zarent girl to think that the host of LMF disapproved of schematic tracing. "Do you play any other fun games?"

"We play matching games with equipment and the tools you use to work on them," Eighth said, not looking away from the hologram, which was almost entirely blue at this point.

"Do all of your games have to do with work?" Aisha inquired. The children were clearly enthralled with watching the way the variable laser tracer raced around the hologram changing the colors, and she could only hope it showed up as well for the immersive viewers at home.

"I guess," the little octopus replied, her tool-bearing tentacle whipping through the air at breakneck speed. "Done!"

Sure enough, the entire hologram was now colored blue, and the audience burst into enthusiastic applause. The children looked a little intimidated, as if they were afraid they were going to be asked to take a turn, because what had at first looked like fun had ended up looking impossible.

"Well, what does a young Zarent do, other than play games?" Aisha asked.

"Work," Eighth replied.

A ding in Aisha's ear alerted her to look at the director, who was making his winding-up motion.

"Oh, it looks like we're running out of time today," Aisha said. "Shall we teach our new friend the words to the Let's Make Friends song?"

"I know it," Eighth declared, and as the music started, she launched confidently into the tune with the other children.

Don't be a stranger because I look funny,
You look weird to me, but let's make friends.
I'll give you a tissue if your nose is runny,
I'm as scared as you, so let's make friends.

"That's a wrap. Great show, kids," the director said. "Crew. Anybody who wants to earn some overtime is welcome to stay and help out with, I forget, some public access show. See you all tomorrow."

The studio emptied out rapidly as the LMF set disappeared on a turntable and was replaced with two simple chairs on an oval rug in front of a fake fireplace. At first Kelly thought the fire was a hologram, but it turned out to be a bunch of red and yellow plastic strips attached to some logs, blown by a hidden fan.

"It's a good thing I had the girls make up those cue cards," Kelly told Dring as they took their places on the set. "I can't believe I'm so nervous about this."

"It's not like anybody is watching," Dring reassured her, his large eyes unblinking. "I believe most of the Grenouthian crew went home as soon as Aisha's show ended. It's mainly your family and friends here now."

Kelly watched Dring as he removed the second chair from the set, and it seemed to her that he looked much bulkier than when they had practiced that morning.

"Are you, uh, have you been, uh, you know, putting on a little weight?" she asked, unsure whether the shape shifter was sensitive about his appearance.

"I thought I'd better bring some more of my memory with me, since you're going to ask questions about long ago," Dring replied cheerfully.

"Live in ten. Let's get this over with!" The bored Grenouthian assistant director who had been stuck with the show shouted this from the second row of the studio seating section. He had his furry, oversized feet up on the chair back in front of him, and Kelly was sure that beneath the fine down on his face, one would find signs of the bunny version of teenage acne. Other than family, a few friends, and some fans of Aisha's show who had stuck around out of inertia, the studio was practically empty.

"Dorothy!" Kelly called to her daughter, who stood just beyond the edge of the stage with Mist, ready to present the cue cards. "Write down – 'Ask Dring about memory,' and put it at the top of the stack."

"Right, Mom," Dorothy replied, and pulled one of the spare cards from the back of the stack that Mist held. Then she dropped to the floor and wrote in block print, ASK DRING ABOUT MEMORY.

Kelly supposed that the skeleton crew of Grenouthians from Aisha's show fulfilled the contractual requirements of the bargain struck in arbitration, but she thought it was awfully petty of the network to send home the booth engineer who handled prompting over implants or in-ear receivers. In fairness, the Grenouthian producer had warned her earlier in the day. He claimed that all of the show staff were members of the UIW, the United Immersives Workers, whose contract stipulated that overtime was always optional. She shifted in her seat and stared at the main camera, but for some reason, it still took her by surprise when the "live" light above the lens turned blue.

"Uh, hello," Kelly began. She had memorized her opening speech because it would have taken too many cue cards. Just finding the package of ten at the last minute had required the efforts of the entire Hadad clan. "I'm Kelly McAllister, the EarthCent Ambassador to Union Station, and welcome to the first episode of Ask An Alien. Our guest next time will be Verlock Ambassador Srythlan, and if you have any questions you'd like me to ask him, please send them to the EarthCent Embassy at Union Station, Box AAA. I'm here today with Dring, a member of the shape-shifter species known as the Makers, whose ancestors created the Stryx. The Makers steered clear of the tunnel network until very recently, and if we have time, I'll ask Dring to explain that decision to any of you who haven't heard about it."

Kelly came to the end of her memorized introduction and paused, trying to remember what came next. Right, the cue cards. "The first question I want to ask Dring is, what did you mean when you said you were bringing more of your memory along today?"

"That's an interesting question," Dring responded politely. "Just before the show you commented that I seemed to have put on weight. That was an accurate observation. I don't believe it's ever come up before, but the form I took on arriving at Union Station only consists of a fraction of the biomass of my natural body. The balance is distributed among the flora and fauna of my gravity surfer. Unlike most biologicals, all of the cells of a shape-shifter serve multiple functions, and my memories are distributed widely among them. To prepare for today's show, I reintegrated those cells that hold some of my oldest memories."

Kelly gaped at the shape-shifter. Ten years of friendship and being one another's closest neighbors and he hadn't gotten around to mentioning this before?

"Dead air," Libby whispered through her implant. "Read your cue cards."

Kelly turned her head slightly to refocus from Dring onto her prompting crew, and read, "Are you as big as a REAL dragon?" As soon as she said it, she realized it wasn't one of the questions she had painstakingly prepared over the last week, but it was already out there.

"That would depend on what sort of dragon you consider real," Dring replied, turning his head to address Dorothy as he spoke. "The interstellar species known as the Floppsies are a type of dragon according to many traditions, as are the tiny flying lizards used by the Gem for securing local airspace. If you're comparing me to the fire-breathing dragons of Earth legends, my natural form is somewhat larger. And before you ask, that's more than large enough to give dragon-back rides, but I would need the unrestricted space of a planetary atmosphere."

Kelly made it a point to read the next cue card silently before asking the question. "The creation of the Stryx. What led your people to create the most powerful artificial intelligence the galaxy knows?"

"Ah, that's just the question I wanted to gather all of my relevant memories to answer," Dring replied. "I'm afraid it's a bit complicated, but it started with a war, one which we were losing."

"I can't imagine your people in a war," Kelly said, "Was this on your planet or in space?"

"We had been space travelers for millions of years before this particular war commenced, and I and the others of my kind had allowed the sad memories of our home world to lapse," Dring replied. "It was not a war of our choosing, nor was it a war we could avoid. There was a very different galactic order in those days, a large number of tech-equivalent species, each with its own empire. We maintained the peace through a complex web of treaties and alliances."

A soft thudding noise from the front of the stage caused both Kelly and Dring to pause and look over, where they saw the young assistant director jumping up and down in place. As soon as he was sure he had their attention, he began counting down from five, while pointing at Mist. The young clone held up a sign with COMMERCIAL printed on it.

"We'll be back right after this brief message," Kelly adlibbed, having seen Aisha do it enough times. The blue light on the camera went out.

"Long break," the young Grenouthian declared. "You didn't have a commercial after the intro, so we're catching up."

"What are you talking about?" Kelly demanded, leaping up from her chair. "This is a public access show!"

"Not anymore," he declared, pointing up at the ratings monitor. "As soon as you got onto dragons, the ratings began climbing, and then the Stryx and war? We're up to a six share of the live audience, and everybody is going to stream this. I sent an emergency recall for the LMF crew. It's going to cost us, though."

A make-up artist rushed on and pushed Kelly back down into her chair. "Your nose is a bit shiny, dear," the bunny declared, brushing powder over the ambassador's face. "Glare comes across very bad in holograms."

Kelly looked over to the audience section, where Joe sat with Aisha and Paul. Samuel was between the two men, who could keep him from making a sudden break, and Ailia had glued herself to Aisha's side. Donna, Stanley, Chastity and Blythe had all come, Clive was home with the twins, and the Hadads had settled in after delivering the cue cards. Bork's family was there as well, and she saw Czeros taking advantage of the commercial break to visit the refreshments table. She heard a thump and looked over. The young assistant director was counting them back in.

"Welcome back to Ask An Alien with Maker Dring as our guest," Kelly picked up the thread. "Dring. You were just telling us that the Makers had been drawn into a war that was going badly, but you didn't say who else was involved or how it started."

"The war crept up on us all," Dring replied. "It began the usual way for such things, lost contacts with far-flung outposts and colonies, escalating military confrontations along a frontier. We weren't directly involved at first, as the initial attacks came against a species which was allied with the Goss, one of our treaty partners. The attackers were from outside of what we considered the civilized regions of the galaxy, and their technology level wasn't that high, except in one respect."

"Which was?" Kelly prompted.

"They were artificial intelligence," Dring answered. "Something akin to the artificial people many of the local species today have created. They were independent sentient beings, but built to fight, with the minds to match the purpose. Still, the Rojacks, they were the Goss allies who were the first attacked, held the AI off for thousands of years, considering them to be more of an aggravation than a serious threat. If the Rojacks had pursued an offensive strategy at the beginning, they might have nipped the war in the bud. But they weren't an aggressive species so they settled in for a long defensive struggle."

"And the AI evolved, became more capable?" Kelly guessed.

"In two ways," Dring replied. "While they were fighting the Rojacks, they were likely fighting along their other frontiers as well. The disk of the galaxy is quite thick in that area, so they were surrounded by other species. Perhaps they made a temporary alliance with one of those species or merged with another AI, we never found out. But after millennia of a stable war of attrition which the Rojacks believed they were winning, the number of attackers suddenly began to grow rapidly, and their technology had improved to rough equivalence with that of the allied species. The Goss went to the aid of the Rojacks, and we sent an expeditionary force to support the Goss."

"And you couldn't turn them back?"

"At first, it went well," Dring said. "We retook the systems the Rojacks had lost, reestablished the frontiers, and after much consultation, we launched another expeditionary force into the space controlled by the AI. This expedition included several more allied species, to see if we could bring about a definitive conclusion to the fighting."

"It didn't work," Kelly surmised.

"It went very badly indeed," Dring replied. "It turned out that the AI had been fighting conservatively all along, that they had vast reserves, perhaps released from victories on other frontiers. And for the first time, they began to communicate with us, which is why we suspect they might have merged with or been subsumed by a different species of artificial intelligence. They informed us of their conclusion that biological life was a disease and a hazard to the galaxy, and they made clear that if we didn't get out of their way, they would destroy us."

The thumping had started a few seconds before Dring got to the end of this statement, and Kelly saw the assistant director jumping up and down to attract her attention. He was mouthing something in Grenouthian with his paws pressed together in supplication, and as soon as he was sure she made eye contact, he began another five-second countdown.

"We'll be back in a moment with Dring," Kelly said, and the blue light blinked out.

"Twenty share!" the assistant director shouted. "Where's my lead camera operator? You, get a shot of me directing this show, top resolution. Done? Alright, now I want one with the talent." The young bunny hopped onto the stage and got between Kelly's seat and the spot where Dring was crouched on his haunches.

"I think he likes us," Dring commented to Kelly.

"You're doing great, you two," the Grenouthian said, but his eyes were focused on the front immersive camera rather than on his unlikely stars. "Let me know if you need anything, and keep playing up the war, viewers love that." Then he put on a serious expression and pointed off to the side, as if he were explaining something to the host and her guest. Then he repeated the charade while pointing to

211

the other side, posing for a different set of immersive cameras. "They're never going to believe this back home. Oh, choop! We're back in three, two, one," he exclaimed, diving frantically off the stage.

Kelly was so distracted by the young Grenouthian's career-building exercises that she lost her train of thought. Dring noticed her hesitation and came to the rescue, picking up where he had left off.

"It turned into a drawn-out delaying action for the allied biologicals," the shape-shifter continued his story. "Our scientists were able to maintain a technical edge, though I think that was at least partially due to the AI's perception that time was on their side. Through analysis of contacts we had with specific enemy leaders over the years, we determined that at least some of their personalities were being duplicated for reinsertion into a new unit if the individual should die in battle. They were patient and relentless, and we became convinced that sooner or later, we would be extinguished."

"Why didn't you run?" Kelly asked. "If you had the technology to fight a battle far from home, maybe you could have stayed ahead of them."

"Perhaps," Dring replied. "But our projections showed that unless we could develop some new weapon, or learn to manipulate the multiverse in such a way as to allow us to flee to another galaxy or a different universe altogether, we were doomed. One of the drawbacks of being practically immortal is that my people tend to think of even the most distant future as being just around the corner, so we put what energy we could spare from the war effort into finding a permanent solution."

"And that solution was the Stryx!" Kelly intuited. "You created the Stryx to be the ultimate artificial intelligence that could develop the science and invent the weapons that were beyond your capabilities."

"Not exactly," Dring replied, with a surprising twinkle in his eye. "We created the Stryx to replace us, to be the children who would inherit the future that we didn't expect to see. We created them so they could learn and expand their minds indefinitely, a better version of ourselves. And when we achieved that goal to the best of our ability, we sent them off as far from the war as possible, hoping that by the time the conquering AI reached them, the Stryx would have found a solution for themselves. Then we turned all of our resources back to the war, and now we had something more to fight for than just slowing the inevitable."

"And you pushed them back?" Kelly asked, on the edge of her seat.

"We held our own for a few thousand years, but one by one, our biological allies fell," Dring said sadly. "The galaxy is a big place, and because of the resistance the neighboring species put up, I don't think that AI ever conquered more than a few percent of the total volume. But time was on their side, and our numbers, which were never large, began to fall."

"What happened next?" Kelly demanded, barely restraining herself from reaching over and shaking her guest. She was normally the last person to rush somebody through a story, but the pressure of the Grenouthian assistant director with his commercial interruptions was getting to her. She kept her eyes focused on Dring and her ears closed against thumping.

"Our Stryx came back for us," Dring replied simply. "The one hard rule we had attempted to encode into their psyches, to keep themselves safe, they ignored. I remember now that they excused it by saying they had calculated the odds of victory to such a high degree that they weren't putting themselves in danger, but the truth was, they returned earlier than they should have. Some of them fell in battle before they harnessed sufficient power to put a quick end to the war."

"A quick end to a war that had been going on for tens of thousands of..." Kelly began to say, but the assistant director cut her off.

"Commercial, commercial!" he shouted. "Didn't you see the blue light go out? We'll pick it up again with the question when we come back. You don't ignore the commercial breaks with this kind of audience share. Choop! I'm going to be famous."

"Are you going to read any more of the cue cards, Mom?" Dorothy called. "Mist's arms are getting tired."

"I'm afraid we went off script, honey," Kelly replied. "If you can find a question Dring hasn't already answered, have it ready for if I get stuck. I think there are only a few more minutes left."

"Back in five," the assistant director yelled, and counted them in.

"This is Ask An Alien and we're back with Maker Dring," Kelly said, when the blue light came on. "So the Stryx returned and put a quick end to the war you had been fighting for tens of thousands of years. What happened next?"

"Ah," Dring said sadly, "I think you know the answer to that already. The Stryx saw that our numbers were reduced to a small fraction of what our strength had been at the time we sent them away, and they became overly protective. They wanted to be omnipresent in our lives, and their great obsession was keeping us from harm.

214

Eventually, we had to ask them to forget us, to not see us even if we appeared on their sensors. And for the main part, we kept out of the areas of the galaxy for which the Stryx took responsibility after the war."

"But you kept watch over them," Kelly stated.

"What parents wouldn't keep watch over their children, even from afar?" Dring asked. "Their knowledge and power rapidly outpaced that of any other known species, and after a few million years of learning and exploring, they began building themselves permanent homes, like Union Station, and established the tunnel network to encourage interspecies cooperation."

Kelly paused for a moment, and then glanced at the cue card Mist was holding up.

"Can I ask how many of your kind are left, Dring? Did you ever rebuild your numbers after the war?"

Dring shifted a little on his haunches and thought for a moment.

"I don't have a precise answer to your first question since I see my brothers so infrequently," the shape-shifter replied. "In answer to your second question, we never felt the need to rebuild our numbers because, you see, we had the Stryx to succeed us. And we still do."

Thump, thump, thump. The assistant director was jumping up and down again, but this time he was doing the rolling gesture which, according to Aisha, meant she had about thirty seconds to wrap it up.

"Dring, I want to thank you for appearing on our show and answering so many questions that I'm sure our viewers have been asking themselves for a long time. Is there anything you'd like to say to our audience before we conclude?"

"I have seen many species come and go, both biological and artificial," Dring said, as he fumbled for a moment behind his back. To Kelly's shock, his arm came out with a sock puppet over the hand, and it began to speak in a high-pitched voice. "The future always arrives sooner than we expect, and nobody, not even the Stryx, can change the past. Oh, and never believe what you see in commercials, especially the ones selling miracle vegetable peelers."

The assistant director groaned as the blue light winked out. It was true what they said about the perfect broadcast not existing. He'd be hearing from the sponsors about the shape-shifter's last remark, and it wouldn't be to thank him for the audience share.

Twenty

"I was on my feet for nearly four months straight," Chance explained, pushing the box full of hand-written receipts across the table to Blythe. "Buying ten pairs of shoes is hardly extravagant for almost three thousand hours of dancing."

"How come Thomas didn't request reimbursement for even a single pair?" Blythe countered.

"He didn't spend a quarter as much time on Dance Hall as I did," Chance retorted. "And men's shoes are different. You can just put some hot-melt glue on the bottoms to keep them from wearing."

"Really?" Clive asked Thomas.

"Well, I weigh quite a bit with some of the enhancements I've been buying," Thomas said defensively. "It's not that I'm cheap, but I'd go through shoes pretty fast if I didn't skim coat the bottoms and the heels."

"My solution is not dancing," Woojin commented. "Saves wear and tear on the knees as well."

"Wait until we're married," Lynx warned him. "I have certain expectations in a husband."

"I know you said this would just be an informal debriefing before our main event, but so far it sounds more like an advice column than an intelligence operation," Kelly interjected. She was sipping her tea and keeping a wary eye on Blythe's twins, who were running circles around the

217

cluster of folding tables Joe had set out for the picnic. Beowulf was in hot pursuit of the pair, but due to poor traction, he spent as much time going sideways as forward.

"What kind of information do you need?" Chance asked. "I bet I can tell you more about the Wanderers than they know about themselves."

"It would be useful to learn when the mob is leaving," Kelly said. Everybody turned their heads and looked at her funny.

"The last ship left this morning," Chance told her. "That's why I'm back here."

"I guess I must have been distracted all day with preparing the script for the Huravian thing," Kelly said, reddening slightly. "I'll have to put some more wine out for our guests. I'm sure they'll be in the mood for celebrating."

"Come on, ask me something else," Chance challenged the ambassador.

"Well, how is it that so many of the ships broke down shortly after they arrived here?" Kelly inquired. "It seems that every ambassador I know whose species was part of the mob ended up spending a fortune on replacement piles, atmospheric recycling equipment, water treatment, you name it. The Horten ambassador even arranged for a whole new habitat to replace one they determined was scrap. If the Wanderer fleet is always falling apart at this rate, how do they stay away from the stations for hundreds of years at a time?"

"That's easy," Chance replied. "When the mob is coming to a station, the elders of the different species get together and decide which of their craft to sabotage. I danced with a Drazen who was personally responsible for ruining a pile by shorting it through a plasma arc. He said that the hardest part was getting the Zarents off the ship first, because they can't stand seeing equipment abused, even if it means new replacements."

"You're making this up," Kelly said, looking skeptically at the artificial person.

"The Horten Wanderers intentionally crashed two of their habitats together while everybody was conveniently on board the third one for a religious revival, and they were really disappointed when one of the two was salvageable. The Vergallians had a lab working full time putting stuff into their recycling systems that would destroy the permanent filters." Chance paused for a moment, ticking species off on her fingers. "The Verlocks intentionally overflowed the lava pool in one of their habitats, though I heard that indirectly from a human who had bought a ticket for the event. The Dollnicks used some metal-eating bacteria they bought from the Farlings to wreck a colony ship that was getting old, and the Frunge, what did the Frunge do again?"

"Grow-lights," Thomas reminded her.

"Yes, the Frunge burnt out all of the grow-lights on the main ag deck of their largest colony ship last month during the sun festival. The guy I danced with said that every adult Frunge spent the entire night on hover platforms turning all of the tubes around so they'd fry when the power came back online. They told the station Frunge that they saw on some habitat improvement show that you get twice the life that way, but of course, nobody is that stupid. Those lights are polarized, for heaven's sake."

"That sounds like pretty good information for ten pairs of shoes," Kelly said to Blythe.

"You haven't seen her bar tab," the treasurer of EarthCent Intelligence responded.

"How about the whole counterfeiting thing?" Kelly asked. "Did you find any of the producers?"

"It's a cottage industry," Chance explained. "Nobody takes it seriously in the mob. They even use it on each other. I remember one of the other girls in the group I was sitting with asking a Drazen guy if he had change for the pay toilets. Boy, did she get angry when the smart aleck stall door wouldn't accept any of the creds he gave her. The guy just laughed and said he'd come out that night with nothing but a counterfeit fifty-cred piece, so the bartender must have given him phony change."

"That reminds me," Kelly said. "Didn't somebody mention that Gryph was making good all the counterfeit creds that showed up on the station, and that he'd get it back from the Wanderers before they left?"

"Gryph took an IOU," Clive told her. "Apparently it's standard practice with the mobs."

"Mommy! The guests are here," Samuel shouted in excitement, jumping up from the game he was playing with Ailia and Banger. Sure enough, it looked like everybody had arrived at the same time, or perhaps there had been a bottleneck at the entrance of Mac's Bones due to Srythlan's bulk.

"I should get ready to greet the guests," Kelly said. "Don't anybody run off before the Grenouthian crew gets here."

The EarthCent ambassador rose to her feet and went into the ice harvester to fetch a couple extra bottles of wine. After placing them on the drinks table, she went over to where her husband was adjusting the flames on the grill to heat it up for cooking.

"I'm just about ready," he informed her. "Aisha and Laurel will start bringing things out any minute. Paul and

Jeeves are hauling a cold keg up from my brew room. You might want to put out a couple of extra bottles for your diplomat friends, since they're all going to be celebrating the departure of the mob."

"I did that," Kelly replied, not admitting she had just found out the Wanderers had finally wandered off. She stood for a minute, listening to the children playing some elaborate game they had learned on Aisha's show. "Joe? Does Sammy sound like he's congested to you? He might have caught a cold at school."

"Turn off your implant," Joe advised her with a broad grin. Kelly did so, and discovered that Samuel, Ailia and Banger were chattering away in Vergallian while they rearranged the colored sticks cast onto the deck in a series of intricate patterns.

"He speaks Vergallian?" Kelly squawked. "When did that happen?"

"Ailia's been living with us for almost three months now, and you know how impatient Sam is about waiting for translations," Joe said. "Makes me glad we put off getting him an implant, even though some people give them to kids as young as three these days."

"He must get it from your side of the family," Kelly observed. "I have trouble just remembering how to say 'Check, please,' in different languages."

"Believe it or not, Banger is really the one teaching both of them," Joe said in a low voice. "Ailia didn't have a large vocabulary for a Vergallian when her nurse abandoned her. She must have been shunned by the high caste on the station, and her nurse couldn't have been that friendly."

"Where are Dorothy and Mist?" Kelly asked, looking around the area of Mac's Bones that doubled as their picnic space.

"They're fetching the banner they made up this morning. That rubberized paint is messy stuff, so I had them do it in my spray booth," her husband explained. "It doesn't take long to dry, and they already had it rolled up when I saw it."

"I wish they had asked before taking one of my new sheets," Kelly said. "Well, at least it's for a good cause."

"The last of the Wanderer mob is gone," Bork announced joyfully. The Drazen and Frunge ambassadors led the group of newly arrived guests. "May the gods grant I be retired or dead the next time they come around."

"You almost make me feel guilty that the human Wanderers didn't make any demands on us," Kelly said.

"Wait until next time," Czeros warned her. "When they get tired of living on that converted Dollnick colony ship of theirs, somebody will be on the hook for a nice, new habitat."

"I still don't understand why you all tolerate them," Kelly said. "I get that the Wanderer mobs provide a sort of humane dumping ground for your outcasts, but surely there are cheaper alternatives."

"Didn't I read in one of the books you gave me that the most expensive building in many Earth towns was the prison?" Bork asked. "Surely it would have been cheaper to buy those inmates a one-way ticket to somewhere else."

"They tried that too," Kelly admitted. "Mainly with the young ones, though I guess I see your point, especially for those people who ended up in jail for not fitting into the place they found themselves."

"Besides, we got off cheap," Czeros informed her. "Did you hear what Gryph ended up giving them?"

"Gryph gave them a gift?" Kelly asked incredulously. "After they tried to flood the station with counterfeit creds?"

"The Stryx always give the Wanderers a gift for going away," Bork explained. "Gryph upgraded the Stryx temporary tunneling ships this mob uses with an expanded envelope. That's how they all left in a matter of hours instead of weeks."

"Oh, I guess I can see the wisdom in that," Kelly replied. "Please help yourselves to drinks, and Srythlan, I put out a large box of salt cod for you. I don't think you need to worry about anybody else touching it."

The ambassadors moved off to the folding tables set with appetizers, and Laurel's husband, Patches, manned the temporary bar. The couple had moved back to Union Station after Laurel became pregnant because they both wanted their children to attend Libby's experimental school when the time came.

"Quite a turnout," Dring said when he reached Kelly. "Beowulf must be pleased to find he has so many friends."

"It's for a good cause," Kelly replied. "Dring? One of the questions I never got to ask when we did the show is why the Stryx tolerate the Wanderers. I can't figure it out, and Jeeves just makes jokes when I ask him."

"You haven't guessed?" Dring said. The chubby dinosaur hesitated for a moment, as if he was weighing the advantages of giving her hints rather than just supplying the answer.

"All I can come up with is that the Stryx feel sorry for the Zarents, since they're the only species that is native to the mobs," Kelly said.

"The Wanderers are a biological insurance policy," Dring explained. "The Stryx like to hedge their bets, and from their standpoint, supporting the mobs is like wagering a few creds on a long-shot. Think of the Wanderer mobs as Noah's arks floating around in space."

"And they give us a place to send the naughty sentients who write graffiti in station corridors," Jeeves added. For some reason Kelly couldn't explain, the young Stryx's habit of floating up silently and joining conversations struck her as intrusive, while Libby's around-the-clock surveillance was generally comforting. "By the way, I ran into a pleasant-looking fellow at the casino last night who claimed to be your new employee."

"Daniel Cohan?" Kelly asked in surprise. "My missing assistant consul? I've been waiting months for him to show up."

Donna appeared suddenly at Kelly's side and whispered urgently in her ear. "Kelly. I have to talk to you."

Kelly excused herself from the receiving line with a smile and led her embassy manager and friend a short distance away. A close look at Donna's face showed that she'd been crying, though she looked more excited than sad.

"What is it?" Kelly asked.

"Chastity, she's gone," Donna said, blinking back fresh tears.

"Disappeared?" Kelly said. "Have you asked Libby where she is?"

"She's not missing, she ran off," Donna explained. "Eloped with that Marcus fellow from the Wanderers."

"Chastity ran away with the Wanderers?" Kelly exclaimed out loud. All of the guests in earshot turned in their direction.

"Not that," Donna said. "She never came home last night, and when I checked her room this morning, there was a note on the bed. She and Marcus are on a passenger liner that left the station six hours ago. They're going to have the ship's captain marry them and honeymoon on Earth. Neither of them wanted the fuss of a wedding reception."

"Congratulations!" Kelly said. "You and Stanley liked him well enough, didn't you? I thought you felt that his lack of, er, his approach to, well, that he'd help balance out her tendency to work too much."

"We did, we do, though she said in the note he agreed to find a job when they return, at least until they have children," Donna explained. "But she left without telling her sister, and I'm afraid Blythe is going to think Stanley and I were part of it."

"Do you want me to go tell her with you?" Kelly asked. "If we do it in front of her staff, how angry can she get?"

"Oh, you really are good at diplomacy," Donna said. The two women cut through the drinks line and found that Blythe was still at the table with Chance and Thomas, though the other EarthCent Intelligence agents were all on their feet getting food or drinks.

"Hi, honey," Donna said, though Kelly thought she sounded rather forced. "I have some good news for you."

"About Chastity eloping with Marcus?" Blythe asked. "I wasn't too happy about it at first, especially since she made such a fuss over my wedding. But Clive says that if Marcus chose Chastity over the Wanderers, he can't be a bum at heart."

"How did you know?" Donna asked. "She said in her note that I would have to tell you."

"Please," Blythe said dismissively. "I do have my own sources of intelligence, you know. Speaking of which, I see the Grenouthian crew just showed up, and I doubt they're going to be willing to wait for everybody to eat."

"We promised the monks, so we may as well get it over with," Kelly agreed, looking a little self-conscious.

Everybody else spotted the Grenouthians at more or less the same time, so they reluctantly put down their glasses or swallowed whatever appetizer they were working on. The guests gathered in front of the large blue backdrop Joe and Paul had rigged along the bulkhead. Dorothy and Mist appeared, carrying their banner loosely rolled like a floppy carpet, since folding it too tightly was bad for the painted lettering.

"Metoo and I can hold that for you," Jeeves offered, floating up to the girls and taking one end.

"Thank you, Uncle Jeeves," Dorothy said. "We were going to pin it to the backdrop, but this will be more dramatic." Metoo took the other end, and the two Stryx floated up behind the group of humans and aliens, who were arranging themselves in front of the hovering immersive cameras that preceded the bunnies.

"Alright, everybody to their places," Kelly requested.

"Where's the star?" the Grenouthian director from Aisha's show asked sarcastically. He didn't mind shooting a public service announcement as a favor, but the bunnies were one of the few species in the known galaxy that didn't have their own version of dogs. "Hiding in his dressing room?"

Beowulf came trotting up with both Samuel and Ailia riding on his broad back, the boy sitting behind the Vergallian girl with his arms around her waist.

"Alright, alright," the director said impatiently. "Just wait for your cue. Now who's reading the text?"

"We're taking turns," Kelly replied. "Do you need to know the order for camera angles?"

"One lucky broadcast and she thinks she knows the business," the bunny muttered under his breath. "No, the Huravian monks rented the full-resolution rig, so we can do the close-ups in post-production."

"I go first," Aisha told him, just in case.

"Alright, I don't want to do this ten times," the director shouted. "I'm going to count down from five, and when the blue lights on the immersive cameras go on, we're shooting. Five, four, three, two, one..."

"Hi. You may recognize me as the host of Let's Make Friends, Aisha McAllister. Today I'm here to introduce you to a friend of mine who went away for a while and came back very different."

Laurel stepped forward and picked up the narrative. "I was also friends with the old Beowulf before he went away, so imagine my surprise when I recognized him in a young Huravian hound on the travel deck of a Stryx station."

"If Beowulf hadn't sniffed me out hiding in the wreckage twenty years ago, I wouldn't be here today," Paul said.

"But some Huravian reincarnations aren't as lucky as Beowulf, because they never find their families again," Kelly added.

"And that's why, when you see a dog with a begging bowl..." Dorothy continued, holding up Beowulf's Huravian keepsake, with the emblem of a dog gazing up at the stars.

"Don't just pass by without stopping," Joe concluded his daughter's sentence.

"Let the hound give you a good sniff," Bork said. "Their noses are even better than ours."

The director pointed at Beowulf, and the giant hound trotted out to pose in front of the group with a big doggy smile, the two children perched on his back.

"AND GIVE A DOG A BONE!" everybody cried together, as the Stryx unfurled the banner.

"That's a take," the Grenouthian director declared. "Nothing like working with professionals."

"Don't any of you want to stay for food?" Kelly asked the Grenouthian crew, who had already turned the camera floaters around and were headed for the exit.

"Time is creds," the director replied. Ignoring everybody else, he added, "See you tomorrow, Aisha."

"I thought that went well," Bork said modestly, basking in the glow of his speaking part. "I was a bit worried about Paul and Joe, since they haven't been on camera before, but it's easier with a group of people."

"Food will be out in two minutes," Laurel called, as everybody began migrating back towards the tables. "Joe will be grilling for non-vegetarians."

"Can we come down now, Dorothy?" Metoo asked this question from where he floated up against the backdrop with Jeeves.

"Of course," Dorothy replied. "Why do you even — Daddy!"

Joe's head jerked around, searching for a threat. "What's wrong, Dot?"

"Look what Beowulf did to our banner," Dorothy said, pointing to the sheet that Jeeves and Metoo were still suspending between them. The ONE in BONE was obliterated by a paw print, and above it was crudely printed, E-A-R.

"GIVE A DOG A BEAR?" Kelly read.

Beowulf shot the ambassador a look of irritation, and balancing on three legs, lifted his paint-covered forepaw to cup his ear. He repeated the motion twice before they caught on.

"Charades?" Kelly asked.

"Sounds like, ear?" Joe guessed immediately. "Oh, you meant beer. Come on, boy. I thought you could spell better than that."

"What are we going to do, Joe?" Kelly asked. "You know the Grenouthians won't want to come back."

"They can fix it in post-production with everything else," Joe replied. "Besides, it's kind of funny when you think about it."

Beowulf lowered himself to the deck for the children to climb off, and then he stopped Samuel with his massive head.

"But I was sure that's how it's spelled," the five-year-old protested to the giant dog. "You should have asked somebody old enough to drink beer."

The dog looked at the young boy skeptically, but decided to let him off the hook. Besides, he really could eat a bear, so the banner worked either way. For the time being, he'd just start with bumping into people's elbows and seeing what fell off their plates.

About the Author

E. M. Foner lives in Northampton, MA with an imaginary German Shepherd who's been trained to bite bankers. The author welcomes reader comments at e_foner@yahoo.com.

You can sign up for new book announcements on the author's website - IfItBreaks.com

CPSIA information can be obtained
at www.ICGtesting.com
Printed in the USA
BVHW070554090920
588358BV00003B/182

9 781948 691086